JOHNNY ROCKET

SURPRISE RETURN
TO
SOUTH MIDDLE SCHOOL

Matthew Botsford

DESTINY IMAGE EUROPE
Via Maiella, 1
66020 San Giovanni Teatino (Ch) - Italy
ISBN: 88-89127-25-2

For Worldwide Distribution
Printed in the U.S.A.

1 2 3 4 5 6 7 8/10 09 08 07 06

This book and all other Destiny Image Europe books are available at Christian bookstores and distributors worldwide.

To order products, or for any other correspondence:

DESTINY IMAGE EUROPE
Via Acquacorrente, 6
65123 - Pescara - Italy
Tel. +39 085 4716623 - Fax: +39 085 4716622
E-mail: info@eurodestinyimage.com

Or reach us on the Internet:
www.eurodestinyimage.com

Dedication

To my beloved wife, Nancy, for without your tireless love and support, I would never have been able to accept, much less complete, this stage of this ongoing assignment from the Lord. I love you my friend...my love...my wife...my confidant...and more.

My prayer for you is that the Lord continues using you in His ways more and more, as He talks with you, taking you to His intimate places, trusting you as He does. I am an ever prosperous, ever grateful man because of His gift to me in the form of you.

Table of Contents

⫷ 1 ⫸

Home Again

Johnny yelled in delight at the sight of his trusted mate, T-Dog, speeding across the tarmac through the floating blades of grass, dirt, and dust in the storm created from the spaceship Regatta's touchdown and landing. The surface levelers came to rest firmly on top of the ground.

"T-Dog!" Johnny hollered in delight as the white racer hit him full on, knocking Johnny to his back.

"RRRhhh…mmmhhhh," she enthusiastically sounded, lapping up Johnny Rocket's neck and face with all the affection she could muster.

"Oh, girl," Johnny exuded, "I sure did miss you too." Johnny did his best to speak through all the wet kisses and moist-tongue greetings from his loyal mate, T-Dog. "It's been a couple days since we played, huh?" he said looking into her brownish eyes. "Seems like a lifetime though."

When the dust settled from the canine love attack, Johnny looked back to see his copilot, Leapin' from La Podia, and his Guardian at arms, Vasgus, making their way down the landing

1

ramp, laden with the gear they figured they'd be needing for their recreation time on Earth.

"You guys plan on stayin' awhile?" Johnny asked inquisitively, already knowing full well what their answer was going to be.

"What da' ya mean there, Cap?" Leapin' responded, squinting in the light of the day, making a poor attempt at blocking the sun out of his sensitive eyes with one of his not-too-free webbed hands.

The guys weren't used to the sun's intensity. Being cooped up in the Regatta in the deep of space had forced the comrades' vision to accommodate to the lower light levels. The sky this day was bright blue, streaked with thin white clouds positioned high in the atmosphere. Johnny felt the hot midafternoon sun gleaming down on his back as he continued to play with his four-legged friend.

"I thought you said we were gonna get some downtime when we reached Earth," Leapin' whined.

"Yeah, I know, guys," Johnny replied, not fully answering the question at hand. Johnny called his trusted canine friend back to him. "Sit, girl," he said. "What's that on your collar?" he asked inquisitively, as if T-Dog could respond.

As he gently grasped her by the gruff and collar with one hand and used the other to cup the pendant dangling below her chin, Johnny got his crewmen's attention. "Hey guys, check out how this thing reflects the sun." The boys in the Faith directed their sights as their Captain had asked. "My folks must have bought it for her while we were gone. My mom is always supporting charities for cancer and orphans." Johnny tried to make out the fine inscription on the front of the pendant but had little success.

Leapin' exclaimed, "I wish it was that LBF thing you have been talking about so much, so we wouldn't have had to leave this comfortable planet in the first place."

Leapin' proceeded to smooth his webbed hands through the lush green grass he had paced over to. Repeating himself, Leapin' whined again, "We wouldn't have had to risk our lives and endured all that loud grumbling of those tall Palaveriens— Oreaus and all!" Leapin' was wearing a disappointed grimace on his face. He had Johnny's full attention at this point in his speech and so he continued, "Like the earthquake, the landslide, and Babbling Becky's efforts to kill us—or with that thing that absorbed our whole ship on...what planet was it? Asteroidious? What did you call that thing, Captain? Crater Eaters, I think? And how about..."

"Okay, okay, little buddy. That's enough of that," the Captain cut Leapin' off. Leapin' was really getting wound up and gesturing with his thin, wiry arms all over the place. Johnny continued to speak while getting up from his cross-legged position on the ground. "Just think if we had not gone, you would not have this new gentle giant of a friend Vasgus standing here with you."

Johnny slapped Vas on the back with a resounding thud, only to sting his own hand. "If it weren't for the search for the 'LBF thing,' as you so eloquently put it," Johnny gave a kind sneer to his little buddy, Leapin', "Vasgus wouldn't be standing here with us right now. And Oreaus..." Johnny added, "she saved our lives from that nemeses, Babbling Becky. If it weren't for Oreaus, we all might still be stuck a foot deep in the ground Babbling was morphing with on the planet Palaver."

"Yeah, yeah, I get it already," Leapin' conceded.

"Just think," added Captain Johnny, "of the great adventure you would have missed out on—we all would have missed out on—if we hadn't gone." Johnny pointed at each of his shipmates respectively.

(Recall the exciting adventures "Johnny Rocket and his comrades in the Faith" had in their last mission searching for the Liquid Blue Fuel—LBF for short on planets; Strobia, Palaver, Ecclesiatious, and Asteroidious. Upon seeing a bright blue heart pendant donned by a neighbor girl that seemed to self illuminate Johnny Rocket's keen, creative imagination led him to believe if the source could be found it could revolutionize the world's fuel and allow for endless play time for their Game Kid handheld gaming devices. Nevertheless they soon discovered much more in the way of Power in Jesus and the Holy Ghost.)

Leapin' still showed signs of uncertainty with the whole deal, fumbling about a bit. *Well, the Captain is the Captain,* Leapin' reminded himself, softly kneading his webbed hands inside one another, his thin parallel lips wriggling about.

"Okay, guys," announced the Captain, "let's engage the cloak and go home for some rest. Our own beds will feel real good after sleeping in those metal bunks on the Regatta. And I don't know how long my interactive holograms of Leapin' and myself will fool my parents. I can only put so many action directives and responses in the software programming. It's not quite as advanced as AI (Artificial Intelligence) is, but darn close. And it's not like I can put a Spirit or a Soul in these hologram things so that they can be more human-like."

Looking up toward the Heavens, Johnny continued, "There's only one Creator who can actually create life and His name is God." The Captain was showing some hints of frustration as he turned to Vasgus, the Guardian of Strobia. "Vasgus, I don't think I can hide you anywhere. You're just too big to pass for any grown-up man from this planet that I know of, and you don't look like any wild animal that I've seen. I think if we tried to say you were that Sasquatch Bigfoot thing from the woods, we might get more attention than we want...photographers and the like." Johnny pretended to have a camera in his hand, making clicking noises as if he were a photographer.

"So..." as he stuffed his hands deep into his worn, blue-jean back pockets, "for the time being, maybe you can hide out in the Regatta, eh?"

"Sure thing, Cap," Vasgus agreed with an added head nod of acknowledgement. "There's a few things in there to keep me busy until you both get out of...what did you call it, Cap? School?"

"Yeah, big guy...school," Johnny affirmed with a quick snap of his fingers like a "greaser" from the '50s. The only thing he lacked was the slick black leather jacket to cover his plain T shirt and some hair gel to slick down his rascally dark hair.

With a silent look of affirmation from each comrade to the other, the three broke their huddle they had formed. Vasgus made way for the boarding ramp into the Regatta and its steel bunks, and the other two comrades in the Faith made their way home to the Captain's house anticipating the softness of a real mattress beneath their tired backs, for the time being, "and a time," as the Captain always referred to their stay on Earth.

Leapin' walked silently alongside his Captain, all the time wondering why, or better yet, where that nemeses, Babbling, had gone to. He never saw her, even once, after VeeGee the virtual navigator took over the landing protocols. "Hmm," he silently moaned as they continued the wayward walk to Johnny's abode. *I wonder what Johnny's talk did for her?* He rubbed the softness under his chin while walking along and reminiscing about the Captain's explanation of the Lord and the Word of God that he had told Babbling about. Continuing under his breath, he murmured, "It seems like I'm the only one that notices she's missing in action. How is that possible?"

⟨ 2 ⟩

School Again

The class bell, positioned high above the dusty, green chalk-board, rang the 30-second warning that it was time for class to begin. It also declared that if anyone was still in the hall-way or tardy for class, they would be sent directly to the Principalis' office. The children were very aware that his office was the area of discipline, the fabled dungeon located behind the thickly frosted glass doorway with "PRINCIPALIS" emblazoned in black block letters across the top center of the glass. Only one way led in or out, and that was down a seemingly never-ending, dimly-lit, empty corridor. The school air was filled with the scuf-fling of feet, slamming of metal locker doors, and the chattering of students of every race and creed, size, and shape.

Rebecca Sage took her seat amongst the last of the pupils to enter the room, which was her way of protesting being told what to do by the established system. It was a tactic she had learned from her father one Saturday afternoon. She also made certain she was situated in such a way that she could survey the entire room. As she did so, she spotted Johnny Rocket wearing one of his red and white, wide-striped T-shirts, having the audacity to be proudly perched on the center seat of the front row. His arms were folded atop the creamy colored laminate desktop, his eyes were fixed upon the chalkboard, and his brown hair was spiked up attentively.

"What is *he* doing here?" she spouted out loud with disdain, furrowing her eyebrows in disgust. *He should have been disposed of by Babbling Becky somewhere far, far away, in some distant galaxy or stranded on some inhospitable planet where nothing but man-eating animals live. No doubt, he is anxiously awaiting the teacher,* she thought to herself. *How disgusting,* she cringed. Then she noticed a blob of spittle—hers—on her desk directly in front of her. She wiped it away with her right hand. It was all she could do not to holler aloud, so she agonized internally like a wild beast with its leg caught in a steel trap.

She imagined herself foaming at the mouth and tearing at the desk that contained her. *If only I could get one swipe at Johnny's red-and-white checked back with my dark red-clawed paw,* she envisioned. *This time, I will take care of him myself,* she determined. A vigorous tapping upon the chalkboard snapped her from her dreamland.

"Okay, pupils, everybody pull out their writing exercises and pass them forward," demanded the teacher in a voice too soft for Miss Rebecca Sage to consider obeying. It had no force, no strength.

"I can't take it anymore!" she growled and burst forth from the confines of the puny wooden desk, scattering wood splinters and causing her neighboring classmates to duck in fear as she lunged toward her unsuspecting prey—Johnny Rocket.

The essence of surprise smells so sweet I can taste it, she thought, licking her pale lips as she galloped on all fours like a grizzly bear, her massive red-clawed paws gouging the tiled floor, and muscle-throbbing forearms perspiring from the effort. She was determined to rise up on her two mighty rear legs and tear Johnny to shreds with her powerful front endowments. The thought of complete annihilation of her prey brought laughter and total satisfaction.

"Rebecca...Miss Rebecca Sage..." harkened a voice from the front of the classroom. "Sit up!" it demanded. "If you don't begin to pay better attention during class, I will have to send you to the Principalis," the stern voice warned, putting a period on the end with a clenched fist landing upon the dusty green chalkboard surface. All the pupils responded to the harkening and adjusted their postures to textbook form.

"That's better," the voice complimented. "Now," the teacher's voice softened a bit, "how about those assignments I asked for?" A rustling of papers echoed through the air as one pupil after another forwarded their single-sheet assignment toward the front of the classroom, accompanied by some low murmurs and a few audible, "Quit it" and "Here's mine," plus a couple "I didn't know she could get so 'bad to the bone,' did you?" Some shrugged their small shoulders in response. Miss Rebecca Sage reluctantly complied, knowing full well that a visit to the Principalis would not serve her cause very well at this point.

The teacher grasped the short stacks from the clutched grips of the pupils seated in the front row, in a left to right fashion, and gathered them into one pile upon her four-legged, rectangular wooden desk, which happened to be positioned off-right center from the entrance door so that she could view the pupils coming and going.

Suddenly, the recess bell rang. Its brassy intensity demanded that all pupils exit the building, and usually startled every boy and girl in the classroom. "This is it!" Rebecca deemed, unaffected by the clanging sounds. "I will have my plan fulfilled. I will begin by ridding myself of that obviously incompetent Babbling Becky, and then I will finish the job myself," she snarled with such deviousness she almost surprised herself, stifling her mouth with an open-palmed hand.

Quickly and quietly, Rebecca sauntered through the children to the front of the class, hoping to quickly find Babbling's assignment on the teacher's desk, even though she had not seen her in class yet. She breathed a sigh of sweet victory when she located it halfway down the pile, and stuffed it into her canvas backpack, which she didn't even bother to re-zip. Slinging it roughly over her right shoulder, Rebecca made her way back to her seat and with silent amusement, she watched the other students mill about, in her estimation, like insignificant worker bees. Laughing inside, she thought to herself, *An unfinished homework assignment will surely send her to the Principalis for a while. In the meantime, I must complete stage two on Johnny Rocket,* keeping certain to draw no attention to herself.

"Oh Johnny," Rebecca heralded crescendo-like from the rear of the class. When she got no immediate response from Johnny, she reframed her call. "Johnny Rocket!" she barked. "Won't you wait up for me?" she added with a cutesy smile. "It's been…what?…a couple days since I last saw you, right? I've been missing you," she mused under her breath. "Maybe we can talk during recess?" she pleaded.

At this point, Johnny wasn't sure what to make of Rebecca, and the proverbial wheels were turning in her head.

Johnny leaned against the side of the door jam waiting for Rebecca to come from the back of the class as she had called to him so sweetly. He had heard her the entire time she was trying to gain his attention, but he had coolly chosen not to respond. She was sounding so girlish in her pleas for his response, and it grated on him. As the classroom of impatient children exited for a recess, it left the area quiet. Rebecca's shoes, however, were no longer quiet. Her long eager strides caused her black and tans to make a sound clapping noise with each step. From her perspective she felt like she had grown taller or that Johnny was seemingly smaller, as she quickly approached.

Her soft, delicate smile turned downward at one corner of her mouth, obviously reflecting some of her deceitful thoughts and Machiavellian plans. Miss Sage stopped about three long strides from Johnny as he faced her straightway, leaning with his back against the metal door jam. He could feel the cold metal jam through his thin cotton shirt so he clasped his hands behind his back to insulate himself from the pressure.

"What's up?" Johnny asked Rebecca ever so coolly. Rebecca's eyes narrowed but she did not respond. "You okay?" Johnny asked, seeing the slight change in her countenance.

Rebecca's arms hung down straight at her sides. Her forearms and hands were enveloped in the deep pleats of her shin-length, plaid wool skirt. Johnny heard the obvious sound of cracking knuckles somewhere deep inside those pleats. But nothing was said, nothing seen. Rebecca stood staunchly upright. A thickly weaved, crème-colored sweater that complimented her multicolored wool skirt hung about her broad shoulders with a white, wide-collared shirt beneath the loosely tied sweater.

"What are you lookin' at?" she barked.

"Huh?" Johnny responded. "What am I looking at? I don't get it. I don't know what you're talking about,"

"Don't give me that. I know what you're really like," Rebecca sneered.

"What?" Johnny replied, even more perplexed.

"Oh, forget about it," Rebecca stammered, as she thought to herself, *I'm gonna blow it if I don't learn to control myself.* Then she determined as much as possible to maintain a friendly countenance with Johnny Rocket.

"Hey," she commanded but in a lighter tone, "how 'bout we go down and get a candy bar before we go out for recess? I'll buy it since you've been gone for a couple days," she offered. Continuing in a sultry kind of way, she exclaimed, "They've got that favorite one of yours…what's it called? A chocolate peanut butter buster bar?" Rebecca overexaggerated her gestures, revealing soft hands and flowing movements.

"Well…" Johnny contemplated, and finally answered, "I don't see why not." He then added, "We've got plenty of time, and it *has* been such a long time since I've had one of those candy bars. They just don't have any vending machines out in space yet. Maybe that's something to think about next," Johnny concluded with a snicker.

"Great! Let's go then," Rebecca eagerly prodded, intentionally ignoring the "out in space" comment.

Just as Rebecca had smoothly placed her right arm around Johnny's shoulder, Leapin' came bounding in, and with a grunt sidled himself between Johnny Rocket and Rebecca, to the obvious disgust of Rebecca.

"Hey guys," Leapin' loudly announced, eagerly peering up at the two of them. "Where ya off to?" he asked, cocking his head from side to side and lifting an eye toward each side respectively. "Isn't recess this way?" Leapin' pointed one of his long green affixed fingers in the opposite direction of where Rebecca had nonchalantly turned Johnny toward.

"She's buying me one of those chocolate peanut butter buster bars," Johnny exclaimed. "You know, Leap. My favorite one." Johnny got this dreamy look on his face and continued, "It's thick and chocolaty on the outside, and then it has crunchy peanut butter inside. It's been such a long time since I had one of those babies," Johnny moaned and rubbed his belly.

"Yeah, well, maybe next time, Boss," Leapin' redirected his friend. "Right, now I got something better for you. Sorry, Miss Sage, I'm a-gonna have to take the Captain here off your hands. We appreciate your kind offer. Maybe some other time."

"Hey! Wait a minute there, little guy," scolded Rebecca. "I told your *Captain* here," she mused about the "Captain" part, "that I would buy him a chocolate peanut butter buster bar, and that's just what I intend to do." Rebecca then reached between them, and grabbing hold of Leapin's right shoulder, she pried him out of their midst with enough strength and force that he popped out from between the two of them and crashed into the nearby locker wall.

12

"Hey now!" Johnny scolded. "There's no need for that, Rebecca," Johnny scowled.

All of a sudden, from down the hall came a booming voice, startling the three of them from their antics.

"Hey, you guys!" boomed the call, now a little closer than before. "What's goin' on?"

It was Vasgus. "I thought we were going to meet during your recess?" inquired the mighty Guardian of the planet Strobia. "You guys goin' out for recess, or what? Come on. Time's wastin'. The teach' will be calling you guys back in shortly, and I've got some other stuff to attend to. Like you always tell us, Captain, for everything there is a season, right? And right now the time is for us to go to recess so we can talk...privately." The mighty Vasgus emphasized the word "privately" as he glared down at Rebecca Sage.

"Sorry, Miss Sage," the Guardian empathized. "Johnny's got an appointment to keep with his fellow crewmen...outside."

Upon the insistence of his crewmen, Johnny Rocket pried himself from Rebecca's tightening grip and grabbed hold of Leapin's arm. The two joined Vasgus already a couple steps away.

Rebecca was livid as she watched as her prey confidently walked away, flanked by the towering figure Vasgus on his left and the shorter Leapin' on his right. She continued to watch as the three comrades reached the exit doorway. Then step by step, they descended down and out of Miss Sage's line of sight, with the immense one, Vasgus stooping to get through the school doors.

"Ohhh," she growled out loud, simultaneously pounding her clenched fists into the sides of her thighs with a muffled thud. "That Johnny Rocket is really getting on my nerves; and those other two—Leapin' from that stupid planet La Podia and the new guy...what's his name? Vasgus?" Rebecca shuffled her position to the left, and planted both hands on her wooly hips. "It's that new guy I'm most concerned about after seeing what just happened. He may just present a serious problem. Those two never seem to be very far away from Johnny, their dear Captain," Rebecca spouted and sneered with contempt. "I've got to figure out a way to get to Johnny Rocket."

Out on the playground, Vasgus beckoned to the Captain, "Hey, Captain, what's next for us to do?"

"I'm glad you asked, Vas. It's a brand new mystery for us to solve," Johnny answered, exploding with excitement.

"Hopefully we can solve it *and* remain on the ground," Leapin' countered.

"Well, I don't know about that," Johnny answered, "but...okay guys, it goes like this," Johnny began his explanation.

"The intent of our last flight was to discover where this LBF might be, right? As we went from planet to planet searching for the LBF, we found that *we* were the ones that had something *they* needed." Johnny paused while looking into the somewhat perplexed faces of his friends and then continued his rhetoric. "It was *our* Faith," he emphasized. Continuing on, Johnny explained, "Our Faith was the something that the peoples needed, right?" raising his eyebrows at his comrades. "Our Faith in Jesus Christ and His ability to bring real, lasting change to them."

"Yeah?" Leapin' cried out with a question in his voice.

"So...that's what I'm saying," Johnny boldly continued. "We first went looking for the LBF to change the world in a good way."

"It's still not a bad idea," Vasgus interrupted in his baritone Strobian voice.

"Yeah, that's right, Vas," commended the Captain. "It's still a good idea because like I said before, it will revolutionize the world's fuel, especially the video games like Game Kid that we have. So," Johnny emphasized, "we still have to find it, but we have an additional objective this time 'round, right?"

"I guess so," Leapin' replied under his breath, but loud enough so the other comrades in the Faith could hear him.

⌐ 3 ⌐

Spy Trouble

By this time, Rebecca Sage had made her way out to the playground for the short remainder of recess and approached the three comrades in the Faith. She wasn't running; however, her strides were long and purposeful, and her feet raised some dust as she went forward. "Hey!" she shouted as she neared them. Figuring she was still too far away, she waited a moment or two until she was almost within earshot before she continued to yell, "You guys think you're pretty smart, gangin' up on me in the hallway like that, don't cha? Well, what about now that I'm ready, standing right in front of ya?" Rebecca posed.

"Ready for what?" Johnny responded incredulously.

"For what I've got planned next," she responded, her face reddening.

Suddenly the back-to-class bell rang, inciting a riot of swarming children back through the propped-open, double metal doors, up a small flight of stairs, and into the hallways.

"Well, we'll talk to ya later, Rebecca," Johnny said as he brushed by her heading into school behind all the other students.

15

"Yeah, we'll talk to ya later. C'mon Vas, class is about to start," Leapin' proposed, feeling the tenseness in the air.

"Uh-uh, little buddy. I don't go to class, remember?" Vasgus replied. "I'm not from here. I, the Guardian of Strobia," he bellowed and thumped his barrel chest, obviously proud of what he was.

"Yeah, yeah, I remember. It's not often you let me forget," chided Leapin'. "But, what are you gonna do while the Captain and I finish up the school day, huh, big guy?"

"I'm gonna do a little work inside the Regatta and run some navigational checks that the Captain asked of me...ya know, after the last misadventure due to navigational problems."

"Yeah, but Vas," Leapin' added, "those navigation problems weren't caused by any equipment failure; they were caused by that Babbling Becky thing."

"I know, little buddy, I know. However, the Captain wants me to install some additional safety features into the programming software to make unauthorized tampering or access into the navigational grids all the more difficult. Apparently, voice print analysis and matching aren't enough in this day of technological advancements, even with the high artificial intelligence levels of VeeGee, our virtual navigator," concluded Vasgus.

"So, what are ya goin' ta do?" Leapin' asked, amazed at the intelligence of his gigantic friend.

"I'm not sure yet, Leap, but I will once I get in there. I always know what to do once I get my head and hands on something," he replied, sounding confident in his Strobian abilities. Then as an afterthought, he said to himself, *I am trained in the ways of the Ancient Guardians, ya know.*

Rebecca Sage hadn't left the playground and was standing, unbeknownst to the boys, within earshot where she could clearly hear their discussion. She then began to ponder, *I've got to get into the ship when Vasgus goes in. I must see what I have to do differently this time just in case I can't get rid of Johnny during school.*

…Now, how am I going to get on board without Vasgus seeing me? Maybe I can get close enough to see the electronic combination he uses to enter the ramp door when he goes on board.

She continued to brainstorm. *Come to think of it…I don't even have to get close. All I have to do is get within 100 yards. My virtual photo-binoculars can zoom right in and take a picture just as the mighty Guardian is keying in the code.* Rebecca laughed menacingly to herself. She could taste victory in her plans.

She looked around carefully to make sure Vasgus hadn't left for the ship Regatta yet and then spied him leaning up against the far slide ladder. *He must be thinking about what he is going to do to make the ship's navigational systems more secure. It looks like he's fumbling with his thumbs.* She scowled and wondered, *Maybe he's not so smart after all?* However, there was one thing Rebecca didn't know, and that is Strobians have exhibited a high intellectual capacity for eons in their endeavors of waging successful war campaigns.

I better get a move on it if I want to be able to get those binocs before he enters the code when I'm not there, Rebecca worried to herself. So she began her sprint home, remaining unconcerned of school attendance, fostered by her belief that it was an institution which was imposed upon her by people she didn't even know anyhow. And any concern that a classmate would see her stepping off campus paled in comparison with the anticipation of victory she was feeling.

Like an Olympic champion she ran on this humid spring day. "Gotta get home. Gotta get home. Gotta get home," she repeated under her heavy breathing the whole way until she reached her driveway, then slowed to a brisk walk. The length of the black asphalt drive, cracked with age and spotted with tufts of green and brown grasses, seemed extra long today. She jumped up the wide wooden stairway leading to her front door, and her hard-soled shoes slapped soundly on each of the worn and peeled, grey-painted steps.

Reaching for the tarnished brass doorknob, she jumped as she noticed her dad suspiciously peering through one of the thick, rectangular, pane-glass windows of the grey and white wooden door. The door flung in as she grasped for the doorknob.

Her father's deep raspy voice hit her loudly. "Just where do you think you're going in such a big hurry, girl?"

Rebecca responded timidly after catching her breath—not from the long-distance marathon-style run, but from the scare her dad gave her the moment she saw him peering through the window pane.

"Hi, Daddy. You're home early today. Did they give you the afternoon off from the mill?"

Her father glared down at her as she stood startled in the doorway. "Since when did you become the lady of the house?" her father barked.

"Daddy?" Rebecca replied, not understanding her father's rage at such a simple question. Continuing, her father roared, "Your mother used to be like that when she was around. She always had to ask questions. 'Why are you doing that? Why are you doing this? What are you doing about that? What are you going to do about this? How will we ever make it?' "

Rebecca's dad was very animated as he spouted off; his arms flailing and face grimacing. "'You know,'" she would say, "'Rebecca will need a good education someday and by then college will be even more expensive. Have you ever thought about that? What about this bill? It's already past due! Don't you ever think about anything besides yourself?'" He slammed his clenched fists down on the dark oak table in the kitchen with a sound thud. His eyes began to cloud up.

Rebecca neared her father, sliding up next to him and whispered softly, "Daddy, its okay. I'm glad you're home."

"Thanks, Honey," his tone softened. "I didn't mean you any harm. Forgive me? It's just that your mother could get sooo...ohh...sooo..." The pupils of his eyes darkened to pinpoints as the rage returned. He drew up his fists, tightly clenched to his chest.

Rebecca quickly responded, "You know I do, Daddy."

"I know, Darling," he acknowledged and added, "You're quick at that. You're the best child a dad could ever ask for. Your mom just didn't seem to understand me like you do."

"Oh, Daddy, you're always saying that to me."

"Well, Honey, it's true."

With that last comment Rebecca's dad leaned over and planted a big kiss firmly upon her soft left cheek. "Uh...Dad?" Rebecca softly mouthed.

"Yeah, Honey," he replied in a more comfortable tone of voice. "I hope you don't mind, Daddy, but I have to get going."

"Sure thing," he replied, and then added with a series of affirmative nods, "Remember Honey, whatever you need."

"I need to run up to my room before I go out," Rebecca answered. Then she turned quickly and bounded up the carpeted stairs to her room decorated in pink with satin-ruffle drapes adorning the wide, leaded-glass windows.

Slamming open her double-wide louver closet doors, she stretched to the top shelf and retrieved the photo-binocs. *Now all I have to do is get to the ship before Vasgus, snap a shot of him doing the pin number on the keypad, and then I can go back later when nobody is around and set up my own sabotage techniques. That way I won't have to rely on someone else to do my work. That someone else mainly being Babbling Becky, wherever she is hiding herself these days,* Rebecca concluded her thoughts.

Quickly correcting herself out loud, "Oh yeah," she giggled, "that's right...she's probably on her way deep into the Principalis' office by now."

Rebecca huffed down the carpeted stairway, barged by her father, hollered a spry, "See ya, Daddy!" then flew through the half-closed doorway, skipped down the wooden steps, and hit the asphalt driveway at full speed.

"Whew! These kids got a lotta energy these days," her dad commented as he rescued the door from denting the wall and pulled it into a closed and locked position.

☆ ☆ ☆

Back at South Middle School, the bell had just rung dismissing the pupils from school for the day. Leapin' strode to the front of the class just as Johnny was beginning to get up from his desk.

"Hey, Cap? Do ya think Vas is finished with his updates yet?"

"No, Leap, probably not yet. I told him to wait until he heard the school bell before he started to walk to the Regatta to do his work. That way we shouldn't be too far behind him. You know how he can get when he really gets into a job. The next thing ya know he's rewiring the entire ship."

The boys looked at each other, shrugged their shoulders, and kind of laughed. "Oh, well," added the Captain, "without him, we certainly would have been doomed or marooned many times."

"Yup," agreed Leapin'. "Maybe even dead."

"We better get going. Let me get the rest of my stuff," Johnny informed his copilot.

"Right behind ya, Cap."

So, the two of them sauntered out of class, toting their respective backpacks loaded with school goodies. They proceeded down the hall toward the doors with the bright red exit sign illuminated above the pupils—above everybody, that is, except for the mighty Guardian of Strobia.

☆ ☆ ☆

Meanwhile, hidden behind the dense foliage of the surrounding hedges, Rebecca Sage snickered as she fumbled through her backpack trying to locate the photo-binocs.

"Jeez, that hurts," Rebecca whined as she became caught in a thorny hedge while fumbling about. "Finally," she groaned, exasperated with all the searching. "Patience has not always been a virtue of mine," she added, bringing the photo-binocs up before her eyes. "There it is!" she spouted, zeroing in on the ship Regatta. "Now all I have to do is wait for the mighty Vasgus to show up and show me right in."

Moments later she saw Vasgus approaching from her right. As he neared the Regatta's starboard tailfin, he paused, then looked to his rear and to either side. "Ha!" Rebecca cried out and then immediately muffled her cry of glee with both hands. "I've got to be more careful," she expressed under her breath. "Besides being as strong as a bulldozer, that Vasgus probably has other heightened abilities that my normal, earthly adversaries don't have, like extra-normal hearing or something stupid like that." Rebecca ducked lower in the shrub upon her next thought—*Maybe the same goes for his vision too.*

After the mighty Guardian appeased his sense of safety and secrecy, he came around the tailfin to the fore of the ship. He paused once again, which brought another grimacing blurt from Rebecca. "Oh, come on! Can't you tell, oh mighty one, that you weren't followed. Get on with your business already," she finished impatiently.

Vasgus then came to the port of center of the ominous whale-shaped ship, extended his right hand, opened-palmed, to the port-sided tailfin. Suddenly, with a swishing sound heard all the way back to the thorny bush area of Miss Sage's hideout, a keypad appeared, eliciting an "Ahh!" from the dear Miss Rebecca. "Finally," she exuded. "Now just move your big fat hand out of the way so I can see the buttons you press to get in that fish ship of yours," she spoke aloud, obviously unconcerned at this point about being quiet.

As Vasgus began to methodically depress a combination of buttons, Rebecca peered through her photo-binocs and began to fine-tune each eyepiece, enhancing the clarity of Vasgus' thick fingers. "Jeez," she exclaimed, "they don't pay much attention to cuticle hygiene on that planet Strobia, do they?" She snorted, "Now I've just got to be sure to record the sequence of the combination for playback later." Rebecca hit the red record button on her binocs and began recording the swift but deliberate movements of the mighty Vasgus.

She adjusted the right eyepiece to make up for her reduced vision in that eye. As a young child she had been hit in the eye by a dirt ball while throwing mud balls at a neighbor kid. Rebecca reminisced, "That kid so deserved to be mud-balled. And I can't believe that I'm the one that got caught and grounded for a month for picking on poor little Johnny." The corners of her mouth turned down as she mockingly pouted, "Ohh, that burns me up to this day. I even got a raspberry in my eye, which I have to live with forever."

Rebecca was beginning to incite herself into a fuming rage. "Not him though. He's fine. But now I'll get back at him. Ha! I'm gonna get his pride and joy—his precious ship, the Regatta.... That's right, Vasgus, go on in and do your stuff. I'll be back in a little while," Rebecca guaranteed herself.

She figured she didn't need to waste her precious time waiting for him to do whatever it was he was supposed to do inside the Regatta. "Besides, it won't do you any good; I'll figure it out," Rebecca mocked. My time is better spent stopping at Freezees for an ice cream and getting one of those double-scooped homemade cones with hot fudge dripping down the sides—the ones where they have to wrap the bottom of the cone with a napkin to soak up the excess fudge before it drips on your hand." So, Miss Rebecca Sage made her way out of the park and headed downtown to Freezees Ice Cream Parlor at 4th and Grand.

Crashing open the metal-framed glass doors to Freezees, Rebecca sauntered up to the counter, keeping her eye on the main menu hung high above the glass ice-cream coolers, which were lined up along the sides and rear of the little shop, forming an inviting "U" shape for its customers.

"Well, hello there, little Miss Sage," came a small elderly voice from beneath the counter. "What will it be for you today?"

"Probably her same-ole same-ole," a boy's squeaky voice rudely interjected from the back room. Suddenly, a redheaded boy poked his head through the rectangular opening at the back. "Hey, Beck!" the boy clumsily waived. "What's the good word?"

Rebecca sneered back at the boy whom she determined as unworthy to receive a response.

Directing her attention back to the owner of Freezees, she answered, "Yes, I will have my usual…if you don't mind."

"Oh no, we certainly don't mind," the elderly man answered, shooting a look to his young helper who was not looking through the window any longer. Miss Sage's glance had shot him clear out of the opening and sent him cringing in the back somewhere.

Rebecca looked up noticing a funny-looking, double-scoop, ice cream-cone clock mounted on the wall; the time was getting late. She looked out the window and saw the evening sky fast approaching. *I'm gonna have to get going home soon. I think I'll have to invade the Regatta on another day. Today is not the day. My dad will start to wonder where I am and I don't want to get him all upset with me,* she concluded in her thoughts.

"Will you want this for here or to go?" squeaked the voice of a boy.

"What!" she spouted turning to face the counter and that incredulous little redheaded boy handing her the ice cream with a devilish grin across his freckled face.

He repeated as smoothly as his young vocal chords could allow, "Will you want this for here or to go?"

"Don't even think about it," Rebecca resounded like thunder.

"What?!" he asked, acting totally baffled by Rebecca's response, but knowing deep down in his heart exactly what she was talking about.

"You know what I'm talkin' about," Rebecca growled. "I saw that smirk you gave me from behind the safety of the counter. You know," she began in a softened, almost pitiful kind of way, "that you're not my type," as she flipped her head and hair to the side away from the boy. "I don't like freckles," she finished, arrogantly snatching the ice cream out of his hand, and spinning away and out the door into the evening.

The double-scooped beauty of homemade ice cream and waffle cone disappeared before Rebecca had walked three blocks. On her way home, Rebecca's thoughts turned again to her plan that would ensure that Babbling Becky would soon be visiting the Principalis' office.

"Tomorrow, during school, the teacher will have noticed Babbling's paper missing and will order her straight to the Principalis for disciplining. This teacher doesn't mess around with lame excuses like some others do," she said out loud.

It made her chuckle to herself. She was proud that the things she did always seemed to work out as planned, not like that bungling Babbling Becky with Johnny Rocket. "Hee, hee, hee!" she laughed in a sinister tone striding along the concrete walkway. *And the disciplining that Babbling is going to get will be real good,* she minced over in her mind.

⊂ 4 ⊃
The Intruder

Back at the Regatta, Vasgus had completed his security updates, creating viral-based backdoors that would open up when anyone besides the Captain would attempt to access points. In the past, others aboard the Regatta had had clearance to the navigational systems. Johnny had thought it would be best if it were programmed that way, for personnel operative backup. However, in light of the latest sabotage attempt, the Captain had changed his mind.

Vasgus was pretty proud of the viral-based backdoors he programmed because never before had a virus been utilized in this capacity. They always were something to be avoided, and now he had actually programmed them to work on the ship's behalf. If an unauthorized attempt was made to access the navigational systems, the virus would spawn into the ship's networks, shutting down everything except that which was already in operation. Hence, the Captain's orders could not be changed by anyone but himself, not even by the Navigation Station Operator as Babbling had morphed herself into during her sabotage attempt of Johnny's last mission.

Vasgus began to power-down the Regatta's interior lights, preparing for a good night's rest. He was still trying to get used to the idea of sleeping on a metal bunkbed. On his home planet of Strobia, Vasgus and all the other inhabitants generally slept leaning against a Pyroak tree. It is their sworn duty as they reach adulthood age to protect Strobia and its peoples, and remaining upright lends itself to fulfilling that duty. Only as infants, for the first 20 Earth years or so, do Strobians lie down and rest at night.

Vasgus looked at the tiny bunks and then considered his size. "I can't do it. I just can't lie down." Instead, he chose to go to his usual spot, at the back of the ship, which allowed him easy viewing of the main-entrance doorway. "It's funny," Vasgus thought aloud. "Captain Johnny always says, 'When you've done all that you can do, just stand.' I'm not sure I get it."

Vasgus rubbed his immense square jawbone with a thick-fingered hand. "Yet he lies down and sleeps for hours at a time," Vas pondered with a perplexed look on his face, still holding his jaw with his hand, as if to keep it in place. "Must be a human thing," Vas concluded as he leaned against the interior wall. He then smacked his meaty hands together and the ship's lighting dimmed to a small glow.

After sleeping through the night with dreams of revenge filling her head, Rebecca awoke rested and excited for the school day to begin. She scampered down the stairs, grabbed a breakfast bar and a juice, and gave her pop a kiss on the cheek. He was sitting at the rectangular Formica kitchen table, smoking a Lucky Toss cigarette and drinking a cup of black coffee. "Bye, Daddy. See ya tonight," Rebecca hollered as she went out the door, closing it only halfway in her haste.

"Honey!" Rebecca's dad hollered as the door coasted shut. "So fast?" he questioned, taking a last puff on his dying cigarette peering at the backside of the wooden door, which badly needed painting. *One of these days,* he thought to himself, *I'll get that repainted.*

Rebecca hadn't heard her dad's question and continued her dash down the driveway. All that was going through her mind was how Babbling's discipline in the Principalis' office would go down. Her stride quickened to a gallop in her eagerness, like a small horse or pony at the fair.

Before long, she reached the school grounds and passed by several students, ignoring their hollerings of "Hey, what's the hurry?" One girl beckoned from a small group at the corner of the school property, "Whoa, look who's in a hurry to get to class today," and then they all laughed ferociously.

Rebecca was too focused to pay any attention to the shouts. There were some "hellos" from friends and some not-so "hellos" from some not-so friends, but either way it didn't break Rebecca's cadence. She galloped right up the stairs into the school, jogged left and into the classroom. But to her great displeasure, she found that her usual seat for maximum observation was already taken by some boy whom she coined as pudgy.

Rebecca sneered down at him while swankering by to the next best post of observation. The teacher then briskly strode into the classroom and let her briefcase land soundly upon the wooden desktop, startling many pupils. But not Rebecca—she was too thrilled with the expectation of what was to happen next to Babbling Becky.

Then it happened. The teacher summoned Babbling Becky to the front of the class before the obnoxious bell had a chance to clamor.

"Miss Becky? Could you please come up and see me a moment," the voice called from the front.

Rebecca was not aware that Babbling had been sitting so close to her until she heard the metal-legged chair scrape on the polished tile flooring of the classroom. Rebecca looked up just in time to see Babbling move alongside her. Rebecca thought, *I must be slippin' in my powers of observation. I didn't notice where Babbling was sitting. I have to be more careful—things like that can be devastating in times of war.*

Rebecca consoled herself with the fact that any shortcomings she might be experiencing was probably due to all the stress of this Johnny Rocket thing, which would soon be over. She reassuringly reminded herself, *Just got to get Babbling set up and secure in the Principalis' office. Then at break, I'll go to the Regatta.*

By the time these thoughts were going through Rebecca's head, Babbling had reached the teacher's desk. "He-he," Rebecca giggled under her breath. She couldn't hear what was being said between the teacher and Babbling, but soon enough she was able to deduce that her plan was fast on its way to success.

Babbling slammed her fist down upon the stack of homework assignments and then stormed out the classroom door. Rebecca began to daydream a bit. *I wonder if all those tales are true about the Principalis—the lack of light, the darkness, the sounds that seem to come from out of the walls. It's said the dark is so dark you can't see your hand in front of your face.*

"Okay, class," the teacher beckoned, "that's enough staring. Why don't we go ahead and begin our break early. Remember, since we are taking our break early, it's not the first bell that signals the end of recess, but the second bell. So listen closely," she concluded in her instruction by shaking a finger to emphasize the point.

This is perfect, thought Rebecca. *Not only is Babbling on her way to the Principalis' office, but I've got more time to get to the Regatta.*

Rebecca rushed out into the playground and looked around to see if anyone was watching, particularly a teacher or hall monitor. After determining that no one was paying attention to her or noticing that she was about to leave the school grounds, off she went, across the sidewalk and down the street into a neighboring yard.

The thick green hedgerow bordering the neighbor's finely kept lawn only added to her secrecy as she scampered along. "Ke-he, ke-he," she chuckled to herself. "Come on," she spoke to herself, trying to keep calm. "If you want to get this thing going, ya gotta move faster than this. By the time you get there, that Regatta could well be on its way to take-off and everything would still be messed up." "Yeah, yeah," Rebecca answered, carrying on a conversation with her conscious or alter ego.

In any case, in response to her inner conversations, she picked up the pace en route to the Regatta. As Rebecca rounded the last home of the subdivision, the Regatta's landing pad came into view. "Ahhh," she exhaled, "there it is." Rebecca continued her approach with the stealth of a cheetah hunting its prey—low and slow.

As she approached the landing pad, all that seemed to lay before her was a large clearing of weedy grasses. She immediately recalled that the Regatta was probably in cloak, unlike the other day when she snapped the photos of Vasgus. "All I have to do is find the depression marks in the field and then I will have located one of the Regatta's outriggers. I just gotta be careful not to walk head-on into the ship and hurt myself. I could bang my head on the stupid thing. That's just my luck with the whole mission so far. Get myself knocked out and lay here in the grass for them to find me," Rebecca angrily mumbled. "Ain't gonna happen," she assured herself. "I'm not letting this chance get away. I'm doing things the Rebecca Sage way—my way!"

Stopping in her tracks, Rebecca began to survey the area for impressions or irregular surfaces—any area that would presume to be under some sort of load. "Ahh," she whined out of desperation. A few moments later, about 50 yards from where she was standing, Rebecca saw rectangular areas where the ground seemed to be lower with no grass. "Presumably under one of the Regatta's leveler pads," she thought out loud.

Slowly, Rebecca walked toward the areas she located, periodically putting up her hands in front of her to be certain not to walk into the outside of the ship as she imagined earlier. With her hands positioned straight out in front of her, she looked like she was sleepwalking. All of a sudden, a deafening sound filled the air. "Oh great," she said. "That Vasgus must have set up some kind of perimeter alert and I walked right into it—like being invisible wasn't enough."

She ran away to duck behind a huge nearby oak tree and then heard the hydraulics of an elevator door operating. *Gotta be that Vasgus coming outside. I don't dare peek around and blow my cover,* she thought. Rebecca's tiny frame in comparison to the immense oak tree was well hid as her fingers grasped the bulging chunks of brown bark in great anticipation. Then she heard heavy, thumping, methodical footsteps.

It sounds like Vasgus is walking the perimeter, she thought. Taking shallow breaths, Rebecca couldn't contain her curiosity any longer. Slowly, ever so carefully, she peeked around the massive trunk, at the same time checking all of her other body parts to make sure they remained behind the tree.

Then she saw Vasgus on the far side of the landing area. *Maybe a total distance of a school football field,* she thought. She zeroed in on the only visible part of the Regatta—the elevator door. The sight of the oval-shaped entrance to the Regatta made her heart quicken. Rebecca ducked back behind the oak tree for positive safety. She could feel her heart beating all the way up into her head—throbbing even. "Keep it cool," she reminded herself leaning against the roughness of the bark.

Then she did it. Without a thought or a second glance, Rebecca sprinted out from the safety of the tree and made direct for the ramp of the Regatta, trampling over and through the long grasses between her and the ship. Rebecca ran with such concentration that she didn't notice where Vasgus was positioned or the prickly burs painfully attaching themselves to her low stockings. Fortunately for her, he was still monitoring the far side of the landing field perimeter, about 50 yards from the elevator door.

Grabbing hold of the shiny rails paralleling the steep ramp, she expedited her ascent up the metal-grated steps, pulling frantically at the rails on each side, moving her forward as fast as her wiry legs could carry her. Upon reaching the top of the ramp, Rebecca paused out of sheer bewilderment. Before her eyes was a vast array of mechanized and computerized "stacks." "Stacks" is the only description that would come to her mind, like the bookshelves in the school library standing from floor to ceiling and about as thick too. These stacks, however, were glowing and beaming different alternating colors. She also became aware of some emitting clicking sounds as she walked in and out, around and about, up and down the seemingly endless array of stacks.

Where am I gonna start? was the first thought that entered her mind. *How is that Johnny Rocket able to do these things?* was the second thought. Miffed, Rebecca continued, *Where did a punk kid like Johnny learn to build this stuff and this space-flying ship? And this other guy— Vasgus—just where did Johnny find him?…Anyway, none of that really matters right now; I just have to sabotage this thing somehow.*

She continued to ponder while looking again at the ominous, luminescent stacks. "Ahhh," suddenly it struck her. *These things are all electrical at some level. If a person wants a surefire way to mess up electrical stuff, what do they have to do?* she asked herself, then answered after remembering what happened when she dropped her hair dryer in the bathtub. *Just add water!* she shouted in her head.

While she was using the hair dryer, Rebecca had accidentally dropped it by the bathtub which happened to be full of water. It short-circuited the whole upstairs until her dad could figure out how to reset the house breakers and it ruined her hairdryer too.

Beginning to get a little fidgety about the length of time she was taking inside the Regatta, her conscious started to taunt her with thoughts of destruction that Vasgus would do if he caught her in Captain Johnny's ship. "Oh forget about the water," Rebecca spouted in frustration. "I'm gonna just get a hold of one of these little circuits and pull it out of the board. That surely will delay any take-off plans Johnny may have."

Rebecca then staunchly positioned herself in front of one of the larger, more intricate stacks. "This one's got to have some good stuff in it," she surmised by its many-colored flashings of light and clicking sounds. However, as she reached her hand out, she simultaneously became aware of a red-taped line on the floor just outside of the stack. Immediately, she heard and felt a sizzling vibration on her arm. Calmly and coolly, she remained still, with her arm outstretched and her hand a couple inches from contact with the circuits themselves.

"What could that have been?" she voiced with some concern. "Must've been some sort of computer thing—processing or something. Static, maybe? I just need to reach a little further." Startling her, that same sound and vibration happened again.

"Oh well, I guess it wasn't done processing," she determined. As she continued to reach forward toward her desired goal, with the red-taped line in her lower peripheral view, suddenly, the length of her arm, which extended in beyond the line, vanished. Right before her very eyes, Rebecca witnessed her arm, from elbow to hand, disappear.

Shocked and terrified, she produced an ear-shattering scream, thinking nothing of forfeiting her secrecy with the noise. *Great!* she immediately thought within the next second. Rebecca had to make a decision—and quick. *Surely that enormity of a beast is plodding his way up the ramp even now,* she grimaced. Glancing down, Rebecca again noticed the red-taped strip on the glistening grey floor. *There is something about that taped line,* she concluded. *I better make sure I keep my feet where they are.*

Rebecca firmly planted her feet right next to the outside of the line. She hadn't moved an inch since seeing her arm disappear right in front of her face. As she remained frozen like a mannequin, she asked herself, *Do I dare reach any further in order to get to one of those circuits or not?* Her answer came abruptly as she suddenly heard the heavy plodding of what was sure to be Vasgus coming up the ramp of the Regatta.

"Crimminy," she whispered. Glancing quickly over her left shoulder and not seeing the Guardian just yet, she determined, *Gotta go for it. Might be my last chance…ever.* After sucking in a huge breath through her flared nostrils, Rebecca stabbed in at the circuit board. It was a weird feeling because she couldn't actually see her hand nearing the circuitry, but she still could feel when contact was achieved.

"Wow!" she exclaimed. "That's really cold. Way colder than ice even." Rebecca could feel the minute details of some tiny circuits beneath the palm of her invisible hand. "All I have to do is pull one of these little things out…" she grunted as she grasped her fingers around what felt like an important piece "…and wa-la! Bye-bye Regatta and hello sabotage."

"Ha ha ha hoo hee," she cackled, but not too loudly. An all too familiar feeling, a vibration, the same vibration she felt earlier, began again. This time the vibration increased in its intensity. Rebecca shuddered and instinctively attempted to pull back from the circuit board; however, she could not. Something would not allow her to pull free. She was affixed—stuck.

"What?" she exclaimed out loud. "Stuck? Oooh, that Johnny Rocket." Then, as she raised her other arm up and in front of her to help push herself away from the stack, she watched aghast as that arm began to disappear too. "Ahhhh!" she gasped in feminine desperation.

Rebecca stood tiptoe at the red-taped line on Johnny Rocket's ship with both arms, as far as she could determine, invisible but somehow still in existence. *I can still feel my arms,* she said to herself, but *I cannot remove them from beyond this stupid line. Agghh.*

Suddenly she recalled the mighty Guardian, and at that instant, she thought she felt a heavy presence beside her. She spun urgently to her right so she could at least confront the mighty Vasgus to his face, but as a result, she unintentionally stepped over the red-taped line caused by the immovable position of her arms and upper body.

"Whaa..." she exclaimed. That eerie vibration resumed. Suddenly Rebecca felt herself drawn forward by her chest toward the stack. "Hey!" she screamed, totally abandoning any attempt at secrecy. "Hey! Somebody...somebody help me! Stop this...this thing! Vasgus!" she beckoned. "Oh great Guardian that you're supposed to be...get in here and turn this thing off!"

The vibration continued to rise in its intensity. But no Vasgus showed up. "Now what?" Rebecca pleaded with anyone who could hear her. Rebecca could feel a pull of some sort—an electrical buzzing and vibrating kind-of thing pulling on her chest and neck. Then just as she so dreadfully hoped for, the mighty Guardian Vasgus showed up at the top of the ramp—just in time for him to catch a shadowy glimpse of someone and hear the echoing of Miss Rebecca Sage's pleas of despair.

⟨ 5 ⟩

What Happened?

Hey, big guy!" shouted Captain Johnny as he and Leapin' scrambled up the Regatta's boarding ramp, creating quite the raucous. The boys' arrival served to be very untimely as it spun Vasgus' attention from what he thought he just saw, to his Captain hailing him from the entranceway.

"Vasgus," Johnny called out.

This time, Vasgus quickly responded, "Yeah, Boss, what is it? What's up?"

Leapin', standing bowlegged just behind the Captain barked out, "You okay, Vas? You look kind of confused or something, but I can't tell."

"Well, little guy," Vasgus began to answer his friend, Leapin', "I just got up here myself. I…"

"Oh," Johnny interrupted Vasgus' thoughts. "How did the work go that I asked of you? Finished?"

"Yes indeedy, Cap—just as you desired. I was outside working on the ship perimeter systems and…"

"Outside, Vas?" Captain Johnny interrupted him again, questioning him with a hand on his hip and a perplexed facial expression.

"Yeah, Boss," Vas responded quickly. "I had to go out and check the perimeter fences after making the adjustments inside."

Vas was feeling a little unsettled by the whole situation, even though he had performed, with Guardian precision and specificity, what the Cap had asked of him. And that was to enhance the navigational systems, making unauthorized tampering impossible. The Captain himself was the only one who could now change the navigational trajectories and protocols once the flight plan was instituted.

Vasgus had installed a live, real-time lock-out circuitry system that would respond to Johnny's interface only. This was an addition to the Artificial Intelligence (A.I.) that Johnny had already created in VeeGee, their virtual navigator. Captain Johnny had, in fact, achieved what modern science and technology could not; he merged computer technology with an organic living system for the sole purpose of assisting in navigating the Regatta. Johnny called this feat of his, VeeGee the virtual navigator.

Leapin' had been eyeing Vasgus since boarding the Regatta and asked him again if everything was okay. Leapin's questioning, this time, caught the Captain's attention.

"Leapin'?" Captain Johnny looked intently at his copilot positioned beside him. "You have always proved to be pretty intuitive. Why do you keep asking if our mighty Guardian buddy Vasgus here is okay?" The Captain slapped his big buddy across his broad shoulders while looking into his copilot's eyes.

"I don't know, Cap," Leapin' replied. "It's just that when I came up the ramp earlier, Vasgus had this weird look on his face."

"Eh, you guys," bellowed Vas. "Can ya give a Strobian a break here? So I looked a little different to the little guy here." Vas was addressing both guys, but primarily focusing in on Leapin'.

"I don't know, Vas," added the Captain. "The last time that we felt something was different, we had a morphing-capable saboteur on board who was attempting to destroy all of us. You recall Babbling Becky, right?"

"How could we forget," piped Leapin'.

Johnny added, "The eyes are the windows to the soul."

"What does that mean, and what's that got to do with me?" attacked Vasgus, startling the boys. Vasgus always had somewhat of a frightening demeanor to him, simply due to the enormity of his stature. The sheer size of his physique lent to being confrontational even when he had no such intention. But this moment, Vasgus exercised a little more "intention" than usual.

"Whoa, Vasgus buddy," Johnny cautioned. "What's goin' on here? Is everything okay?" Johnny had even stepped back out of sheer instinct at his new friend's reactions. "Vasgus," Johnny continued, "what's up? Really now, what's up?" Johnny prodded in a way only real buddies can do.

"Well, Cap, I think it's like this. I heard the perimeter alert sound.

"Yeah…?" Johnny encouraged his friend but gave him the space he needed.

"So I went outside the Regatta to check out the perimeter areas."

"Yeah…?" Johnny again encouraged.

"So, I was out there for awhile—it's a large perimeter, ya know."

"Yeah, Vas, I know. Then what? Did something else happen? Did something else go on?" asked the Captain.

"I…I think so. But I'm just not sure. I think while I was out checking the perimeter areas, the ship was breached."

"An intruder!?" hollered Leapin', flapping his thin arms around in the dry air.

Vasgus in his deep voice, stuttering a bit said, "Well, I just don't know for sure." At the moment he spoke those last words, he clasped his face in his broad hands and hung his head low.

"Vas, what're ya doin'?" Johnny spoke.

"Well, it's like this. On my planet, Planet Strobia, I'm trained by the Ancients to be a Guardian."

"Yeah," Johnny acknowledged that he understood. "You mean like a protector of sorts—a sentry or something?"

"Yes, exactly—a protector of the people."

"Vas buddy, it's okay," Johnny obliged.

Vasgus then mounted an unexpected defense before Johnny and Leapin'. "No!" he bellowed tightening every muscle and sinew, sending deep shivers through Johnny and Leapin's bones. "You just don't get it!" Vas loudly proclaimed. "In all my 500 years of being, never have I failed a guard duty, and I'm not going to start today."

Vas slammed his foot down, creating a vibration through the whole ship floor. Leapin' noticed the foot pound, but was more captivated by the "500 years of being" statement. He had heard it before and was well aware of the advanced age of his big buddy, but it continued to shock him nonetheless. "Amazing," he quietly contemplated while he peered intently at Vasgus.

"What are you doing?" Vasgus beckoned to Leapin' noticing his deep stare.

"Wha-what!?" Leapin' stammered. "I was just...looking at you...th-th-that's all. No big deal."

"No," Vasgus bellowed out. "You were looking at me like I had done something wrong."

"No...really, Vas. I was merely looking at you." Leapin' had become more animated in his gestures, which only seemed to raise Vasgus' suspicions of his little buddy's supposed judgment.

"Wait a minute, guys," interrupted the Captain, prying in between with arms extended. "What is this folly? You two look like you're getting ready to tear each other apart, you know, like you're even about to fight." The Captain had a very perplexed look on his face as his shipmates seemed to be reaching an edge. "Wait…just a minute," he hollered with a strained voice. "Vasgus, come outside with me, will ya?" the Captain ordered.

"Sure, Boss."

"Just walk with me, big guy. Come outside for a moment." Turning his head back as he led Vasgus toward the ramp of the Regatta, Johnny said to Leapin', "We'll be right back. Go and check the navigational chair or something. We'll be back in a flash."

"Huh?" Leapin' asked. "Okay…whatever you say, Cap," Leap replied, totally confused about what was going on and why the Captain would tell him to do something so stupid as to check out a chair. So he flapped his feet off and picked a chair in the flight deck to "inspect," simply out of pure obedience.

"Wait a minute," cried Rebecca, baffled by her unknown location. Looking up and down, peering all around, Rebecca saw seemingly unending circuit boards to her front and to her back. Linear stacks surrounded her. "Wait minute!" she scoffed. "Something's different here. Where am I?" she asked herself peering all about. "No red line. What happened to that stupid red-taped line that I was standing at?" she spat staring at the toes of her saddle shoes. "The air feels different…stuffy. And what's that buzzing sound?" She could hear some kind of whirring inside her head, or around her head. She couldn't quite determine what it was or where it was coming from, but she did know it was irritating and seemed to be rising in intensity, similar to what she had experienced when she was standing on her tiptoes at the red-taped line.

Something was definitely different this time though, but she couldn't quite figure it out. The last time she heard the buzzing sounds, she could step slightly back from the red-taped line, and the sounds would decline. This time, however, the sounds seemed to move whichever way she moved. Her frustration continued to mount, and with her increasing frustration she seemed farther removed from reality, from the reality of placing herself just outside the stacks on Johnny's ship in her sabotage attempt.

Outside the spaceship Regatta, the two heroes halted their forward march, and Johnny turned about to face Vasgus with about three feet remaining between the two comrades' feet.

"Now Vasgus, don't get me wrong. I'm not condemning or judging you for anything. And neither is Leapin'. You know him; he always is amazed by how old you are. That's why he was staring at you—not because he was judging you as a failure at your guard duty," the Captain concluded looking deep and peacefully into Vasgus' strained eyes.

Johnny thought it safe, maybe even prudent to stretch forth a hand to console his big buddy, but he received a vigorous swatting away of his hand as it neared Vasgus' body. Johnny wished he could have aimed higher, to his buddy's right shoulder, but because his friend seemed as tall as a single-story building, all that Johnny could count on touching was his friend's midsection.

"Whoa, Vasgus. What's that all about? You're gonna hurt someone doin' that. Ya probably left a bruise on me already," Johnny scolded his buddy's action while rubbing his sore arm with his left hand—'round and 'round till the sting diminished.

"Sorry, Cap," Vasgus began. "It's sort of a reflex, ya know?"

"Okay, Vas, but I'm a little concerned about something."

"What's that?" Vas questioned Johnny.

"This whole Guardian thing might be just a little too much of who you are. I mean, it's a good thing to be the 'Guardian of the Ancients' for your planet Strobia, but I think the 'Guardian' side of it might be just a little too engrained in your psyche, so to speak."

The Captain was speaking very cautiously, unsure of what he was trying to say and definitely not sure of what Vasgus' response was going to be. Johnny figured he might be attacking the very nature of Vasgus and was therefore prepared for some extraordinary retaliation. Running through Johnny's mind was how the ego, the soulish part of the unregenerate man, was in control of Vasgus before Johnny and Leapin' had led him to the Lord after the Angelic visitation back on Vasgus' home planet during that last mission. This questioning might be perceived by his buddy as an inquisition rather than a captainly duty.

"I imagine," Johnny began, "that when you were growing up you were trained to not ever fail. That failure was not an option. In fact, I bet failure even had dire circumstances attached—maybe even dreaded personal consequences or punishments?" the Captain asked raising one eyebrow.

"Yes," Vasgus acknowledged, walking over to lean against one of the ship's outriggers.

Vasgus continued, "When it was discovered that a Guardian had made a mistake on sentry duty, he was ousted for a specific period of time."

"Let me guess," Johnny interrupted, "the worse-er the mistake, the longer the exile?"

"Yup," Vas confirmed. "Sometimes up to 40 days so I...I mean...the Guardian could think about his mistake."

"Vas," Johnny cried out with great excitement breaking his big buddy's solemn moment. "Just think about how great our Daddy is. Instead of judging all of us, He decided to grant one massive Pardon through sacrificing His own Son, Jesus, to die on the Cross once and for all. No judgments of all our past mistakes or sins. And to top it off, He gave us the Holy Spirit...to fill us and empower us with the desire to love Him."

Johnny figured Vas needed this reminder of what the Lord had done for him. "So what's going on?" Johnny asked wholeheartedly of his buddy who was still so solemn. "Do you think somebody got on board while you were doing the perimeter guard patrol or something like that? Do you think somebody or something scampered up the boarding ramp while you were attending to your other duties?" Excitedly, the Captain continued, "Do you think...huh, Vas? Do you think that's what happened?"

Johnny wanted to be sure to validate his buddy during this intense moment of discourse. "You said, when we were back inside, that you heard the perimeter alert go off, and that's why you needed to go outside, leaving the interior unprotected—so that you could check the perimeter," Johnny reminded him. "But what was in your eyes that our little buddy Leapin' was so honed in on...huh?"

Vasgus adjusted his position and then said, "When I had come back up the ramp after completing the perimeter rounds, I thought I caught a glimpse of something."

"A glimpse of what?" Johnny asked inquisitively.

"I'm not sure of exactly what I saw...maybe nothing at all."

"Now, Vasgus," Johnny continued, "if you think you saw something, I bet my last marble that you did. Where exactly do you think you saw what you saw?" Johnny beckoned.

"Over by the stacks," Vasgus answered and motioned with his trunk-like right arm as if they were standing inside the ship rather than on the outside in the perimeter alert area. "When you guys came up the ramp, you kind of startled me because I was intent on investigating the stacks. Anyhow," Vasgus continued staunchly, "the virus program I installed in our virtual navigation systems—VeeGee—should by all means track down and take care of whatever might have been near those stacks. I put a red-taped line on the floor as a reminder to not get too close. I'm not positive of the viruses' capabilities, and I don't know if it has any outreaching capabilities," Vasgus pondered.

"What do you mean by saying 'outreaching capabilities,' Vas?" Johnny asked this question with a grave concern across his usual smooth-toned face.

"It is a new creative technological advance leap," Vasgus responded turning toward his Captain. "Turning something that is inherently bad into something that can be good," Vasgus finished with a grin.

"Heck," Johnny lauded, "almost sounds like how God turns what the enemy means for bad into something good."

"What?" Vasgus asked.

"Yeah, I remember one song from church that says God turns our mourning into dancing and our sorrows into joy."

"How?" the mighty Guardian asked.

"Well, see, it's kind of like this—our Daddy, God, doesn't want His kids—that's you and me," Johnny pointed at the two of them respectively with his index finger and thumb of his right hand, "to wallow around when we can be happy. And that brings us back to you, my big friend."

"Huh?" Vasgus shrugged.

"Yes, please don't think that Leapin' or I feel you have let us down. We don't even know what happened yet, or if anything really happened at all."

"Captain," Vasgus spoke up authoritatively. "I'm certain I saw something!"

"Okay, Vas," replied Johnny. "Then we need to run the new program you installed right away. C'mon, let's get back inside before Leapin' starts to miss us or actually finds something wrong with one of the chairs," Johnny said laughing about the "chair duty" he had assigned his little buddy to.

Doing a military style about-face, the two marched back up the ramp and into the Regatta. "I was beginning to wonder if you two had left me here to do this 'chair assignment' forever," Leapin' whined as the other two stepped back on board the Regatta.

"No, no," Johnny responded affectionately. "Vas and I were just talkin' a bit," he added.

Before Leapin' could go on, the Captain barked the orders, "Vas!"

"Yeah, Boss."

"Hurry and run that new Regatta-friendly virus program. Let's see what's goin' on."

"Aye-aye, Cap," Vas responded like a pirate of the open seas. The only thing he was lacking, characteristically speaking, was a bird perched on his shoulder, a patch on his right eye, and a peg leg with shiny black buckle boots.

Vasgus approached the Navigator's helm in order to begin the viral software deployment. "Captain!" Vas bellowed. "I need your voice input verification in order to begin the viral deployment procedures."

"What's the protocol you've designed, Vas?" Captain Johnny asked.

"Just your voice print," Vas answered. "The only thing the system requires is your voice authentication."

"I just gotta speak?" Johnny answered with a question. "Say anything?" he added.

To Johnny's surprise, VeeGee spoke out, "Voice authentication complete. Initializing viral scans on mark 3—2—1—mark. Viral scans commencing."

"Wow, Vas," Johnny exasperated. "That is impressive. You've synchronized the software with our virtual navigator guy, VeeGee."

"Yeah, Boss," Vasgus affirmed. "It seemed to make the most sense to utilize existing resources and tie into them for this new defense system, making the most of the ship's integration and technological features."

The Captain, while impressed with his friend's accomplishment, noticed a strange whirring sound ever so silently, coming from the stacks.

"Is that normal?" he asked Vas, while cocking his head to one side.

"This is the first time I've gotten' 'er up and runnin', Cap," he replied. "I'm not really sure," Vasgus answered, revealing a perplexed countenance.

"When do you think we will know if it is operating within its designed parameters?" Captain Johnny prodded.

"Let me look at the viral synthesis gauge to see and monitor the rate of viral production we've got going on," replied Vasgus. He then walked over to VeeGee's readouts and paused at the gauges, scanning what was before him.

The complexity of the instrumentation of VeeGee required Vasgus to do some silent meditations. Finally he belted out over his right shoulder, "Hey, Cap…"

"Yeah, Vas, what is it?" "By the rate of virus production, it looks like we've got a big bug inside the ship's stacks."

"What do you mean?" Johnny inquired.

"Well, by the look of the production stream gauges," Vas began, "it appears as if something of an exorbitant nature has breached our defense array. This could possibly be what I had an inkling about when I was drawn outside to investigate the perimeter fence."

"Well, well, would you listen to that talk about a possible breach," Leapin' cried out from the front of the Regatta while taking a seat in one of the chairs he had so thoroughly "investigat-ed" as the Captain had instructed him earlier.

Leapin's tone created an uncomfortable stir inside the Captain's heart. "What are you getting at, little buddy, with a statement like that?" Johnny asked turning to face Leapin' from the helm area.

"It looks like our mighty Guardian does have a sense of humility after all," Leapin' responded.

"Hey…hey," Johnny remarked. "I know things can get a bit tense around this time, but remember; you've got the Holy Ghost inside to show you how to take the higher road and love one another." Captain Johnny narrowed the distance between he and Leapin' and added, "Remember that!" tapping his little buddy on his cool green chest.

The Captain continued, "I sense one of those times when a pressing is coming upon us. Let's not choose the lesser by foregoing our love for one another. Let's choose the greater and embrace the love we have for one another. Amen? Amen!" he emphasized to both his comrades.

Leapin' piped up, "I was just saying that it was good to hear Vasgus say that it, in fact, was possible, I say, possible, that a breach occurred while he was watching the ship. That's all, Cap."

"Okay, Leapin.' It sounded like you were being sarcastic and trying to cast some stones, per se, at our brother Vasgus here."

Johnny had moved over to Vasgus as he was still positioned at VeeGee's instrumentation panel, and he gave him a quick slap across the shoulders.

"Hey!" Vasgus responded solidly. "What was that for?"

"It's 'cause I love ya so much," Johnny explained adding the old-fashioned outstretched arms for visual impact while still speaking. "Remember a faithful saying, guys," Johnny continued, "that whoever among us is free from the crime, let that person throw the first stone. Now, let's get back to this 'big bug' Vas referred to." Johnny directed to his comrades in the Faith.

"If you're telling me that the viral defenses are building up at an astronomical pace, then we have something to be concerned about. Is there a way to get any more detail about what's going on inside of the stacks, Vas?" Johnny asked of his mighty Guardian friend.

Meanwhile, deep inside of somewhere, unknown to the three comrades, was Rebecca Sage.

⊸ 6 ⊷

Rogue Swarm

"Hey. Cut it out. Quit your pushing!" Rebecca cried out in desperation. Rebecca was, as best as she could determine, speaking to an enormous-sized green grasshopper slowly making its way toward her one long leg at a time. "That's close enough! Stop right there!" she commanded with an outstretched arm as if she were directing traffic on a busy city street. "I don't know if you can understand me, but if you can," Rebecca summoned, "realize I'm warning you that if you do not stop, someone's going to get hurt and it won't be me. Get it, Hoppy!" she threatened shaking two clenched fists at the beast-sized bug marching before her.

Cocking her head in bewilderment, Rebecca asked, "What are you, anyway? Aren't you usually out in some farmer's field in some Third World country devastating their crops?" she added sarcastically. Not surprising to her, no answers came forth from this odd creature. It just kept stepping closer to her, marching in a determined fashion, threatening her with its nearing proximity and twitching antennae.

47

As it approached, Rebecca could better see the details of the creature's antennas and hear the eerie whirring sound once again. The very tip of the antennae glowed fluorescent orange in the blackness of the surroundings. Behind the orange bulbous tips, Rebecca noticed coarse brown hairs with some kind of barb on the ends. Her usual cool demeanor was slowly being replaced by fear and dread. And the whirring sound continued but seemed to be off in the distance somewhere. In any case, it was definitely increasing in its intensity and quickly.

Then to Rebecca's disgust, another set of antennas came into view, poking out of the deep darkness that surrounded her, the antennae wiggling about in the blackness before her. Rebecca summoned up a small but poignant voice, "What are you looking for?" No reply—only twitching. And now an extra whirring sound began to fill the air.

Rebecca began to fidget about, unsure for the first time in her young life, of what to do next. Standing motionless, like a molded clay figurine in the depths of the surrounding darkness, she looked downward, eager to see her shiny-shoed feet, but alas, she couldn't see past the fringed hem of her cross-checked skirt. "Ogh!" she worriedly cried out, cringing together her smooth facial features behind her raised gloved hands.

Johnny and Vasgus poured over the instrumentation panels, seeking evidence for the defense mechanisms' insurmountable buildup. "What's this last gauge for, Vas?" Johnny asked, tapping at the raised rectangular shaped glass.

"Ahhheee!" Vasgus bellowed with such glee, it caused Johnny to jump back from the instrumentation panel, fearing he had touched something he shouldn't have. "That's the microscopic viewing scope that we can use to peer inside the viral colony—the Swarm—that's how I refer to them," Vasgus spoke with an eager glint in his broad eyes, pointing down at the gauge Johnny was tapping gingerly with a crooked index finger on his right hand.

48

"The Swarm?" Johnny questioned, giving his buddy a perplexed look while rubbing his smooth chin.

"Yeah, Boss—the Swarm," Vasgus replied confidently.

"Why, Vas?" Johnny repeated raising an eyebrow.

Vasgus answered, "Because the viral-based defenses have the ability to mutate themselves as the conditions require."

"I still don't get it. Why the 'Swarm'?" Johnny continued probing, knowing in his head that full clarification was soon coming if he just kept asking. Persistence had always paid off for him. Even in his Christian life, he could remember the words his preacher spoke when he got saved some years ago: "Now that you've accepted Jesus into your life, persevere in that faith, be steadfast in your beliefs. Even when your friends think your crazy for believing in the things you believe in, *just believe!"*

The gruff sound of Vasgus' voice furthering his explanation of the Swarm interrupted Johnny's thoughts. "What I've done is created something similar to that of the habits of a locust from my planet Strobia," Vasgus explained. "On my planet, locusts begin their life cycle as pretty little green grasshoppers doing nobody any harm." Vasgus animated the small size of the green grasshoppers by spreading apart his thick thumb and index finger about two inches. "However, as they breed and conditions get crowded or the climate turns more savage, they mutate into aggressive, carnivorous creatures that eventually form wings for flying great distances, hence the Swarm is created."

"Ah," Johnny exclaimed, "I'm starting to understand why you call them the 'Swarm.' Okay, now how do we use the scope?" Johnny pursued.

"It's rather simple in its operation," Vasgus responded, "only be sure to have the radiation-shielding lens in place before opening up the eyepiece."

Johnny put a hand on the eyepiece and did as Vasgus had instructed, moving the shielding lens in place with a simple counterclockwise rotation of the lens. The lens unit resembled a telephoto lens from his dad's miniDV camera that Johnny had been permitted to use at special events like birthdays, holidays, or special church functions.

Johnny then stepped closer to gain a better vantage for viewing through the scope. Upon setting his eyes to the scope, he was aghast at what appeared to him. "Vas!" Johnny exclaimed. Before Vas could respond, Johnny added, "What's going on in there? Is there somebody in there?" he hollered out in fright.

"What?" exclaimed Vasgus in bewilderment. "What do you mean, 'Is there somebody in there?' " Vasgus repeated.

Johnny remained fixed to the scope. "Yeah, just like I said—is there somebody in there?"

This time, Vasgus sideswiped the Captain, nearly knocking him to the floor. "Let me in here. Let me see. Let me see what's going on in there!" Vasgus beckoned with a tone of disbelief.

"Wha…" Vas spat.

No longer able to contain himself, Leapin' sprang into the mix. "What's going on, guys? What's in there? What's so interesting that it's got the two of you practically in shock?"

"Vas," the Captain called out, ignoring his little buddy's comment, "do you see what I see? Rebecca Sage from school inside these stacks? How can that be, Vas?" cried the Captain.

Knowing in the pit of his stomach that Vasgus had unleashed a powerful defense mechanism, Captain Johnny realized also that the viral-based Swarm was something beyond anybody's full comprehension. He also was completely aware that Miss Sage, the one who instigated an earlier sabotage attempt, was in the midst of a carnivorous swarm of creatures that no human could ever withstand! The Captain had to do something.

"Vas!" he beckoned. "Stop it! We have to do something. Those things will eat her alive," ranted the Captain.

"Hey, Cap," Vas resounded, "are you sure you want to stop this? You know, she is the one responsible for our near demise on the last mission. She even put that obnoxious being, Babbling

Becky, on board *your* ship," Vasgus emphasized by pointing his plump index finger toward Johnny.

"Yeah, I know, Vas. But I can't stand by and allow her blood to be spilled, if you know what I mean."

"Yeah, I guess I do," Vasgus reluctantly agreed, trying to keep his instinctual Guardian-type responses subdued. In his head, a confrontation of sorts was going on: *Your duty is to protect and guard, even to enact revenge on those who have attacked you,* said the Guardian Voice inside of him.

No. That's not right, countered the voice of the New Man indwelling Vasgus via the Holy Spirit. *You're to show love, kindness, and mercies just as I, the Lord, have shown you. Jesus, the very Son of God, gave up His life that you, Vasgus, may now live eternally. Recite the Scriptures you have memorized: Romans 6:1-6, What shall we say then? Shall we continue in sin, that grace may abound? God forbid. How shall we, that are dead to sin, live any longer therein? Know ye not, that so many of us as were baptized into Jesus Christ were baptized into His death? Therefore we are buried with Him by baptism into death: that like as Christ was raised up from the dead by the glory of the Father, even so we also should walk in newness of life. For if we have been planted together in the likeness of His death, we shall be also in the likeness of His resurrection. Knowing this, that our old man is crucified with Him, that the body of sin might be destroyed, that hence-forth we should not serve sin.*

Vasgus spoke aloud after the inward confrontation had ceased. "I'll need your help to counter the defenses, Captain." Continuing on, Vasgus reminded the Captain, "Only your voice-matching protocol can alter ship systems at this point."

"Affirmative," voiced Johnny.

"VeeGee," Johnny heralded. "Voicing matching protocol number one...now," he commanded of his virtual navigator with a downward wave of his hand, reminiscent of the Indy race car races he had seen on television at the start and finish lines.

Over the comm came the familiar voice of VeeGee, authorizing the Captain's authority, "Matching protocol number one, affirmative."

"Okay, Vas, what's your recommendation at this point? How do we turn off the Swarm? Ya know, call it off?" the Captain clarified, emotionally peaked.

"You guys still haven't told me what's the big deal yet?" Leapin' cried out from the distant rear. "What're ya lookin' at anyways, Captain?" he added.

"We have a complication inside the stacks, the internals of the ship, Leapin'," Johnny finally responded. "You recall Rebecca from school?"

"Oh yes...yes I do," Leapin' answered annoyed. "She's the one that pulled her sneaky moves on you in the hallway and pushed me into the lockers...she won't be soon forgotten."

As Leapin' was making his way toward the Captain, Johnny gave him a stern look. Leapin' quickly added, "But don't get me wrong...I did forgive her." Leapin' was well aware of how unforgiveness affects a person even worse than the original offense does. Harboring unforgiveness has a cyclical effect inherent to its very nature. Leapin' learned about the Spiritual Principle of forgiveness from Johnny when they met on his home planet, La Podia, years ago.

"So you're telling me she's in there?" he smirked, pointing at the viewing scope Johnny and Vasgus were positioned at. "And what's this Swarm thing I keep hearing you guys talking about?"

Johnny responded, "Yes, it is Rebecca inside the stacks of our ship, and our mighty Guardian friend here," Johnny turned to address Vasgus with honor, "has engineered a deadly defense mechanism that is surely going to encounter her at some point and wipe her out."

Johnny's look of admiration turned to that of grave concern. "Swarm her right out of existence. You mean, kill her, Cap?" Leapin' piped up, confusion riddling his face.

"I don't foresee anything else unless we stop the Swarm before it reaches her," Johnny concluded.

Taking Johnny and Leapin' by surprise, Vasgus bellowed out from the instrumentation helm, "Captain! In my configuration of the Swarm, all can be told to cease and desist."

"Well, that's what we got to do then," rallied the Captain. "Tell it to cease…"

"Captain," Vasgus promptly interrupted, "all can be told to cease and desist…except one."

"What!?" hollered Johnny. "What do you mean, 'all but one'?"

"Yeah, that's right," Vasgus affirmed. "The way the Swarm has proven most effective is to be able to control it…"

"Yeah?" Johnny agreed while rubbing his chin and mouth, wondering where his big friend was going with this.

"Except for one," Vasgus interjected and continued to elaborate. "It allows for unprecedented and unpredictable combat styles and scenarios."

"Well, that's just great!" spat the Captain. "What the heck do we do now?" he added.

"Oh no!" added Leapin'. "Ummm, can I propose another question?"

"No!" shouted the Captain to his little buddy, causing him to shrivel down in pain from the sharp quip. Nonetheless, he continued with his question.

"Just how did a human, a girl from your school, a real live person, get herself inside the ship's internals, the stacks? That's like me deciding to go inside my big buddy, Vasgus here." Leapin' pushed up against Vasgus for effect. "How is something like that possible?" Leapin' pushed harder against the big guy's thigh, making little grunts and other unimpressive spouts of airy sounds.

Vasgus peered down at his little friend's futile attempts of strength and looked to the Captain for an explanation of Leapin's funny behavior.

"You know, Vas," Johnny began, "Leapin' might have a good point here."

"Yeah?" Vasgus grunted. "What would that be, besides beginning to agitate me?"

"No, Vas…listen," beckoned Johnny. "Leapin' is asking how in tarnation a physical, organic life form gets inside the ship system's stacks. Right, Leap?" Johnny gave a nod to his little buddy.

"Exactly right!" Leapin' then bounced away from Vasgus' knobby, tree-trunk thigh.

Captain Johnny paced along the perimeter of the stacks, thinking, and all the time peering down at the red-taped line that Vasgus had marked on the Regatta floor. Step after step, with a military style, about-face at the tape's end, continuing in his dogmatic step by step, conscious of not crossing the red-taped line.

"Captain!" hollered Vasgus in a hoarse voice unfamiliar to Johnny. "You…!" Vas hesitated, "You…" he beckoned once more, "got…to…be…more careful!" Vas completed his speech, charging at Johnny, whisking him away from the red-taped line with one mighty left arm.

After smashing into the far wall, Vasgus leaned his Captain against himself, breathing heavily.

"Vasgus!" Johnny shouted through the one-arm bear hug. "What are you doing? Set me down. That hurts."

Vasgus solemnly obliged his Captain's request, shifting his hold on Johnny to gently set him down with two hands just off center of himself.

While brushing down his ruffled shirt, Johnny commanded Vasgus, "Okay, start talking. What was that all about?"

Seeing the severity in his Captain's face, Vasgus didn't waste any time in explaining his actions. "That red-taped line—the one you were so eagerly traipsing along…"

"Yeah, I'm listening. What about it?" Johnny continued to unruffle himself, combing his fingers through his hair and tugging on the belt line of his blue jeans looking to regain the comfort he had before the violent tackle by Vasgus.

"That line," Vasgus continued, "is the safety zone for the viral defense mechanism we've been talking about for the last couple hours. I do not know what would happen if someone were to step inside that line's perimeter," Vasgus finished shrugging up his house-sized shoulders, muscles contracting about his head as if it were in a musculature press. "It is possible," Vasgus picked up, "that since I've created a merging of the viral, software-based, inorganic world with that of the organic—the locusts from Strobia, that a type of vacuum may exist inside the perimeter line—a vacuum of existence that is struggling to be whole, actually sucking in what is organic in nature."

"You mean like a live person?" Leapin' shrieked, horror inscribed all over his oval face.

"Yeah, Buddy," consoled Johnny, "like a live person. Vas, you really frightened me with your aggressive tackle and carry, but I'm sure happy you did it. I'd hate to be the one that tested out your theory on this vacuum area," exclaimed Johnny.

"Just how are we going to quote, unquote, test out Vas' theory, Captain?" beckoned Leapin'. Leapin' still had a look of horror on his face. "If what you guys say is true—that there is somebody inside there," Leapin' pointed to the massive blinking computer bank systems looming before them, "then something's got to be done about it, even if it is that spurge of a girl, Rebecca Sage," he finished exasperatedly.

"Well, what da ya know," bellowed Vasgus, "you have got a soft spot somewhere in that slippery body of yours."

"What!?" Leapin' cried out. "I don't get it. What are you talking about, Vas?" Leapin' sought.

"Leapin' " Johnny spoke, quickly getting in on the conversation. "Don't worry about what Vas was trying to say. We've got some serious figurin' out to do and cannot allow little quips to come between us."

Johnny pierced Vasgus with a stare that shut Vasgus off in his pursuits. "I'm afraid…" Johnny continued.

"Aghh," Leapin' let out an odd sound that drew Johnny's attention to him again.

"…that now is the time," Johnny continued, "for only one alternative."

"Yeah?" Leapin' spat and Vasgus looked on, both comrades waiting on their Captain's next breath of air.

"…that now is the time for…T-Dog," Johnny paused and then exclaimed with an overhead wave of both hands.

⊂ 7 ⊃

Furry Friend Rescue

"Huh?" Vasgus responded, obviously dumbfounded by Johnny's comment.

"What?" Leapin' added, switching his flat feet and expressing his miffed attitude as well.

"Yes," affirmed the Captain. "You guys don't know all of T-Dog's skills, talents, and tricks. Not only is she the most beautiful white shepherd in the neighborhood, but she is also, by far, the most talented in the entire new world."

"Okay," Vasgus emphatically spoke, exhibiting a grin. "What's the abilities of that white dog of yours?"

"Ahh," Johnny nodded with great anticipation. "Let me demonstrate what she can do."

"Ehh?" Leapin' turned in surprise as he and Vasgus tilted their ears to listen to a far-off bark.

"What's that?" the two vocally synchronized. Then a nearby whimper replaced the barking sound. The two comrades in Faith continued to look each other in the face, their Captain standing

57

stoutly before them with his arms crossed abreast. They remained highly perplexed at the sounds and their Captain's actions. Moments later, a bright white, almost radiant form began to materialize in the midst of the three comrades.

"What is that, Captain?" Leapin' asked. "Is that what I think it is? T-Dog?" chirped Leapin' like he had swallowed a hairball.

The form continued to grow brighter and whiter until the well-toned physique of T-Dog became readily identifiable.

"Well, I'll be..." began Vasgus in a tenor tone. "If it isn't that canine creature of yours, Cap."

"Barrrooo!" T-Dog lunged out of obscurity into Johnny Rocket. "Good girl, good girl!" Johnny patted her gently but soundly with both hands respectively on each side of her deep, large ribcage. "You made it!" he squealed with delight. T-Dog's moist pink tongue continuously wagged and lapped at him and the surrounding air. "That's it, girl!" Johnny encouraged. "Check the air for any kind of danger."

"Okay," Vasgus started slowly. "So she can translate from one place to another. So how is that going to help us with this problem?"

"Hold on there!" the Captain retorted, holding out an arm like a crossing guard stopping traffic. "Just hold on a little while longer and you'll find out. You're going to experience firsthand what she will do for us on the inside of the stacks, Vas," Johnny informed while pointing to the stacks themselves.

Vasgus was positioned to the left of T-Dog and his master, Johnny Rocket, as Johnny gave the order. "Okay, T-Dog...now!" Johnny waived his right hand simultaneously snapping his fingers toward the mighty Guardian, Vasgus. T-Dog took one short step toward Vasgus, sat down on her hind quarters, lifted her sleek, white, front, right paw halfway off the ground, and stayed rigid in that position.

"What?" Vasgus belched, looking to the Captain for some sort of explanation to his dog's weird behavior. At that very moment a strange sound began to fill the air. It began as a low frequency rumble, reminiscent of thunder preceding a bad storm. The sound began ascending slowly through the mid-frequency ranges and escalated to a very high-pitch screaming sound accompanied by great pressure.

Very soon after the initial rumble began, it became very, very cold inside the ship, especially around Vasgus, the mighty Guardian.

"Ehh," Vasgus groaned in discomfort, bewildered by the sudden drop in temperature. Johnny knew that Vasgus would be able to withstand subzero temps and that no harm would come to his big buddy while demonstrating one of T-Dog's many talents. Leapin', on the other hand, was feeling quite differently.

"Captain!" Leapin' shrieked. "What's going on? I can't take the cold." Leapin' began vigorously rubbing his thin arms, trying to create some friction heat with little success. "I'm cold-blooded to start with," Leapin' stated.

"Okay, T-Dog, that's enough. Good girl!" Johnny praised T-Dog while patting her soft white head.

"VeeGee," the Captain summoned, spinning on his heels, "warm it back up in here for our little friend, Leapin'."

"Aye-aye, Captain," VeeGee confirmed with his mechanized voice and did as commanded, eliciting a sigh of relief from Leapin' as the temps returned to the norm inside the ship Regatta.

"Wow," Leapin' burst out, rubbing his thin arms up and down, "that was getting *really* cold," he emphasized with a grimace. "Tell me that T-Dog wasn't doing all that?"

"Yuppers," Johnny nodded, glancing proudly down at his trusted canine mate. "That was all T-Dog's doing!" Johnny emphasized with another loving pat on T-Dog's head.

"So..." boomed the mighty Vasgus in all his grandeur, "am I to guess that the plan of action is T-Dog here will translate herself to there?" Vasgus pointed his knubby, round index finger toward the computer stacks and continued talking. "That she'll go in there and then do what?" he asked, airing some doubt regarding Johnny's plan.

Leapin' was jumping around, up and down enthusiastically chanting, "T-Freeze Dog, T-Freeze Dog, T-Freeze Dog". Leapin' danced and danced, "Yeah, Yeah, T–Freeze, Yeah," he concluded in a mighty leap of exuberance high in the air. "The T-Freeze move...wow!" Leap added.

"Yeah, that's right, Leapin'. The T-freeze move," Johnny affirmed.

"Vasgus!" Johnny heralded. "You see, one of T's awesome skills is that she can lower the temperature in a given area with just one touch of her nose," Johnny exclaimed while touching his own nose. "And the thing she touches will freeze solid."

"Wow!" Leapin exclaimed. "That's even better than I first thought."

"Okay, so she is a pretty cool dog, but..." added Vasgus.

Before he could get his complete thought out, Leapin' jumped in, "Oh, that's funny, Vas. 'A pretty cool dog,' you said," Leapin' chuckled inside.

Vasgus picked up like nobody had interrupted him. "...but what is it exactly that T-Dog will do once inside the stacks where Rebecca and the Swarm are?"

"Well," Johnny answered, "what I see her doing is—once inside the stacks and having located the prime targets, she will commence lowering ambient temperatures, thereby slowing the movement of the Swarm." Johnny then looked directly into Vasgus' dark eyes and asked, "Being that they originated from insect DNA, did they retain their cold-blooded nature?"

"That's an affirmative, Captain," Vasgus responded in military swiftness.

"Good," Johnny responded. "Then they will be affected by the low temps. The whole goal is to slow down the Rogue leader enough to prevent it from doing harm to Rebecca Sage and give us time to counteract the self-defense program."

"Let's hope they're still hoppers," added Vasgus, "and not fly-ers yet."

"T-Dog!"

"Barghh," she answered Johnny.

"Are you ready to go in?" Johnny asked.

"Barghh," she responded again, adding an easily identifiable nod of her long white head and black-capped nose.

"What's she saying, Cap?" Leapin' queried.

"That means, 'yes, '" Johnny answered, giving another snap of his index fingers.

T-Dog suddenly leapt into action, prancing toward the stacks. A bright white buzzing tunnel formed with her inside galloping forward, and then with a quiet "baroo" she vanished from view.

"Quick!" Johnny urgently beckoned, waving his guys to come along. "To the viewing scope," he heralded. "Let's see where T-Dog is."

The boys stampeded over to the viewing scope. Vasgus' great stature assured him first place, but out of respect for his Captain, he took one step back and said, "She's all yours, Cap."

Johnny inhaled a deep breath flaring his nostrils. He brushed away some thick stray locks of moist brown hair from his fore-head and rested his brow against the viewing scope guide. "Whew!" he exclaimed.

"What?" cried Leapin'. "You see her?" he added.

"No, not yet," Johnny replied, keeping his head planted firmly against the viewing scope guide.

"How does she know where to go in there?" Vasgus asked, but then continued before the Captain could respond. "It's an aw-ful-ly big place in there, and there's lots of dangers within the dark side of things," he finished.

"Yeah," replied Johnny, "there are lots of dangers in the dark side of things. But T-Dog is very gifted when it comes to working in darkness. She has a keen ability to sniff out danger. She says she can feel it in her bones."

"Ha! Bones," Leapin laughed. "Is that a dog joke? Ya know, bones? Dogs love bones?"

"No, Leap, it' no joke," corrected Johnny. *Must be Leapin's nerves,* he thought to himself. *Sometimes Leapin' makes jokes to find a little comforting laughter for himself,* Johnny added inside his head. Then he continued out loud, "T-Dog's senses are quite keen, and I know she will find just the right place to be." Johnny spoke with enough confidence so that it would affect his crewman.

"Yeah," cried out Leapin' with enthusiasm, clapping together his webbed hands. "I bet she's got that Rogue Swarm cornered as we speak."

Vasgus added a mighty, "Well, all righty then. Let's get on with it." Vasgus clapped his hands together creating a single deep thud sound that got the attention of the other two.

Johnny returned to the viewing scope, and placing both hands behind his back, he started, "Let me see here."

"What da ya got, Cap?" poked Leapin'.

"I think...yup," Johnny confirmed, raising his bushy eyebrows in excitement and great anticipation. "I see her!" he burst.

"Yeah?" Vasgus inquired.

"Yes, I see T-Dog positioning herself by the mid-stacks," Johnny blurted with excitement. "I think she is ready to freeze something."

"What!?" hollered Vasgus, startling Johnny as he viewed what was happening inside.

"How do you know, Cap?" pondered Leapin' verbally.

"Because Leapin', she has sat herself down directly in front of the large mid-stack and has lifted the one paw to the freeze position."

"Whoa!" Vasgus blurted. "You mean to tell me she is about to face that enemy head-on?" Vasgus careened and then added, "By herself?" evidencing a very whimsical face.

Johnny blurted exuberantly, countering the mighty Vasgus' comment. "She's got the Holy Ghost, Leap!" eliciting a shout of glee from his little buddy, Leapin' who was always glad when the Captain pulled him into conversations.

"You felt how T-Dog began to lower the ambient temperature in here evidencing one of her awesome talents, didn't ya, Vas?" questioned the Captain.

"Uh-huh," the Guardian of the Ancients responded, kind of befuddled in his ways.

The Captain continued, "If I would have let her continue to lower the temperature, we'd all been frozen in our tracks before we could do anything to stop her."

"Wow!" Leapin' chirped loudly. "I always get tickled inside when I think about those kinds of cool things different species can do."

"Well, like I've said before, we all have different talents for different reasons. We just gotta remember that the most important talent is *love.*"

As soon as the Captain finished that statement, Vasgus had his own statement to add. "Boy, Captain, that would be a hard one to get over on my planet. It doesn't take much *love* in killing and destroying and protecting."

As soon as he finished speaking, something gave him a stir deep down inside his gut, so much so, that he wrapped both arms and hands about his midsection, groaning. "Erghh, what's that...fire?" Vasgus exclaimed, mystified as he bent over at his enormous, tree-trunk diameter waist. Continuing, he said, "It feels as though a fire is burning in my belly, Cap."

"I'd say Someone is trying to tell you something, big guy," voiced the Captain.

"What do you mean?" asked Leapin'.

63

Answering, Johnny said, "The Someone is the Holy Spirit, guys. I remember my dad telling me that the Holy Spirit often comes upon a person with fire. I thought it was a little crazy when he first said it, but after the things we've seen of God's power on our journeys, I don't doubt it now."

"But why now?" Leapin' asked, looking at his Captain standing by his side, still positioned in close proximity to the instrumentation helm.

"I think several reasons—most of which I do not know. But one might be because Vasgus had just finished telling us *how* love has no place on his planet Strobia."

"So?" said a confused Leapin'.

"So…" continued Johnny, "one of the things the Holy Spirit does in us is convict us of our thoughts, intents, or actions that are contrary to the Word of God, or those things that just don't quite line up with the mandate of love. See, little buddy, we can all choose whatever we want, but is it what God would choose?

"Eh, guys," Vasgus summoned, "this is all well and good and very interesting, but don't you think we should get back to T-Dog and our uninvited bug inside these stacks?"

"Yeah, of course, Vasgus," Johnny spoke. "I never stopped doing so," he added authoritatively, locking eyes with Vas, then turning away toward the viewing scope once again.

"T-Dog should be well on her way to causing the ambient temp in the stacks to freeze that Swarm leader in its tracks. By then, the others should be de-programmed, right, Vas?" asked the Captain.

"Affirmative," Vasgus responded. "The Swarm will obey the cease-and-desist command."

"Good. Then let's have a look inside here." Johnny placed his forehead in the viewing scope. Inside he saw T-Dog repositioning herself after what must have been her pose for exercising her environmental temperature control.

"Hey, Vasgus," Johnny heralded, "can this viewing scope be turned so that I can see in different directions?"

"Sure, Boss," Vasgus answered. "See the joystick to your right?"

"Yep," Johnny noticed the red-knobbed, multibutton joystick.

"Use it like any other joystick to maneuver the sights, Cap. I installed one that you would be familiar with. It's from the flight simulators you guys always run in the sim bay and on your computers at home."

"Thanks, Vas. I'll get down on it…right now!" the Captain exclaimed as he careened the viewing scope several feet to the front of T-Dog's position.

"Ahh," Johnny sighed. "The Rogue Swarm leader is frozen in its tracks, and by the position of its legs, it looks like T-Dog dropped the temp in a hurry."

"You mean, like, the Rogue was in attack mode?" Vasgus inquired.

"Oh, by all means," Johnny answered. "Some of its legs are still in a running position, not even touching the ground—frozen stiff." Johnny animated his speech, miming the running legs with both arms and wiggling his fingers about. "And it's got these front two-leg thingy's high in the air, pointed straight at T-Dog."

"Phew!" Leapin' exasperated. "It must have been a close one for T-Dog, huh Captain?" Leapin' finished while striding over to Johnny to offer some comfort in the form of a gentle pat on the back. Whether his Captain needed it or not, Leapin' felt better after having offered it.

"I don't know about that, Leapin'. She's well able to handle herself in close corners and head-on combat situations. Okay, guys," the Captain rallied. "Let's get on with it. We gotta get in there and help my pup."

The guys looked at each other bewildered by their Captain's statement. It was his idea in the first place to send T-Dog in after

Rebecca Sage and to disarm the Rogue Swarm leader. Their minds reeled while time seemed to stand still.

Then Leapin' busted out, "But Cap, you yourself gave the order to send T-Dog in there. You said she was the most qualified for this task. What happened? Have you gone *boowaybae*, Cap?" (*Boowaybae* is a term from Leapin's home planet often used to describe someone who has gone crazy, or who is behaving irrationally or contradictory to their normal mode of behavior.)

"Captain!" Vasgus shouted, evidencing his annoyance with the whole thing. "Captain, are you going to stand before us and tell us that after all that has been done, we've got to go in there? I agree with Leapin' here and whatever that word was he said—'boobae'? It's a crazy thought to send one of us in there. Even the mighty Guardian that I am would not dare such a thing. Now that the Rogue Swarm leader is incapacitated, the next logical military tactical response is to destroy it."

"And just how do you suppose we do that, oh mighty Guardian that you say you are?" penetrated the Captain.

"It's really very simple, Captain," admonished Vasgus. "You see, now that T-Dog's got the Rogue immobilized, all we have to do is tell her to dismantle the probes before her."

"What?!" Johnny exclaimed in horror.

"Yeah, those two 'thingy's', as you so eloquently put it, which are pointed straight at her, are the Rogue's probes."

"Probes, Vas?" questioned the Captain.

"Yeah, or as you might say; they are its central nervous system controllers. By dismantling them, the Rogue is useless. Without them, there is no way for the Rogue to assimilate data and thereby formulate militaristic strategic battle plans."

"It's like cutting off the body from the brain?" assumed Johnny.

Vas nodded in great affirmation.

"Without our brain," Johnny said, solidly rapping on the top of his forehead, "we'd be nothing more than blobs of flesh." Johnny pretended to flop and collapse to the floor. "My dad once told me that people who don't look to Jesus as the Head often act like the tail or just blobs of flesh as they go through life. So explain to me how it is 'so simple' for T-Dog to cut off the brains on the Rogue Swarm leader, Vas?"

Vasgus answered, "She needs only to exert side pressure, and they will snap right off."

"You mean to tell me all she's got to do is push on the frozen thingy's sideways, and they'll break off?" questioned Johnny.

"Yep, that's it. That's all she's got to do, Cap," Vasgus affirmed.

"Sounds a little risky to me," piped up Leapin' from behind the guys. "What if it starts to wake up?" he asked.

Johnny gave a concerned look toward Vasgus as Vasgus responded in a funny Australian dialect, "No worries, mates. Now that the Rogue is fast asleep—frozen like, T-Dog can do anything she wants to it."

"Okay, Vas," agreed the Captain, albeit his voice evidenced his reluctance. He felt there was no other choice. And this plan did seem to be the *logical* conclusion to his earlier plans for T-Dog. "I'll give the order to VeeGee."

"Vee," announced the Captain, "prepare delivery of internal system directive to T-Dog."

"Affirmative," Vee responded with monotonic accuracy across the airways.

"Disarm antennae," ordered the Captain into the air.

"10-4. Disarm antennae disseminated into ship's stacks for T-Dog," VeeGee confirmed.

The Captain sighed heavily at the sound of his order and walked briskly to the viewing scope to monitor T-Dog's progress and situation. He switched on the audio inside the stacks as soon as he saw T-Dog moving into position by the Rogue's antennae. As always, the loyal friend, T-Dog, wasted no time in edging up against one of the Rogues "thingy's" with the broad of her white right shoulder.

"That a girl," Johnny said under his breath.

Leapin's highly tuned hearing picked up the Captain's encouraging words and added his own, "You go, girl. Break that thing apart."

Johnny watched as T-Dog's shoulder muscles tensed and flexed beneath her smooth white coat as she exerted more and more pressure upon the frozen beast. Eagerly waiting to see and hear a snapping sound of success, the Captain continued to hold his breath.

Then it came—the snap he had been waiting for. However, at the moment of the snap, T-Dog howled. It was a howl of great agony as she fell to the ground silent and perfectly still. Her four legs lay parallel, two by two.

"My God!" Johnny hollered. "T-Dog's dead. My dog's dead!"

"What?" exclaimed Leapin' in disbelief. "What did you say? Dead? What?!" shouted Leapin' at the Captain.

"Vasgus," Leapin' beckoned. "What's going on? What's the Captain talking about. Dead?"

Vasgus ran over to the Captain, peering down into Johnny's fear-stricken face and asked, "What's going on in there?"

Johnny somehow pressed through his agony and answered, "T-Dog was pushing against the antennae like you said to do. It broke. Then she howled and dropped straight to the floor, and she hasn't moved since."

Johnny was giving a look to his big buddy that required an answer—promptly. But before Vas responded, he had to take a look into the viewing scope for himself.

"Hmm," Vasgus sighed without emotion while peering into the viewing scope.

"What, Vas?" scolded the Captain. "What do you mean, 'hmm'? My dog is lying there right before your eyes, on her side, motionless. Who knows how much pain she just endured and all you have to say is 'hmm'? I've got an injured friend...possibly a dead one, and you're saying, 'hmm'?"

"Captain," Leapin interjected forcefully. "Captain, slow down until we get all the facts, okay?" Leapin' looked up into the face of Vasgus who had since stood up from the viewing scope and said to him in a very captainly sort of way, "Vasgus, what have we at this point?"

Before Vasgus could respond to Leapin's authoritative question, Johnny spoke, "Let me at that viewing scope."

Vasgus made certain to leave plenty of room for his Captain to do as he wished. He complied immediately, stepping way back, arms extended outward.

Johnny took a deep breath and affixed his sight through the viewing scope, bracing his hands on each side of the scope for support, fearing what he would find inside.

But what he saw took away his breath even more completely than the first horror. Johnny cried out so fiercely and forcefully that his comrades were driven back a couple steps. Leapin' looked to Vasgus while Vasgus peered down at his little buddy, Leapin', both blank in the face, not daring to speak.

Then Johnny cried out a second time like fire had hit him from a blast furnace. There, before his very eyes, was his trusted mate of the past five years, not lying on her side dead, but up on her white feet seemingly looking right into Johnny's eyes, her pink tongue hanging out dripping with moisture—as if nothing ever happened—like Johnny had dreamed the whole thing.

Johnny fell back from his position at the viewing scope shocked. "How can this be? I saw T-Dog dead on her side, long legs lying stretched out straight. Not moving, not even breathing… dead," Johnny emphasized.

Johnny turned to his right rear, looking to Vasgus for some answers since his creature-made friend for self-defense mechanisms was Vasgus' creation in the first place. The only thing Vasgus could say was, "Assuredly, I tell you, Cap, that this Rogue must be stopped."

"What has that got to do with what happened to my dog and the question at hand, Vas?" Johnny responded.

Vasgus continued, "It has everything to do with what has by all probabilities occurred."

"Go on," Johnny encouraged, rolling his right hand towards himself trying to increase the dissemination of information from Vasgus.

"Obviously what has happened has to do with Swarm shocks."

"What?" Johnny questioned, taken aback by yet something else he did not know about.

"Yeah, Swarm shocks occur from an indirect physical encounter with the antennae of a Swarm," Vasgus continued. "In this case, T-Dog most likely got shocked as she applied enough pressure to snap off the Rogue's antennae. ... The antennae *is* snapped off, right, Captain?" the mighty Guardian asked in his baritone voice exemplifying some concern on his massive, deeply grained face.

Vasgus knew in his heart the seriousness of the trouble that T-Dog could be in if the Rogue's antennae was not disabled, incapacitating the Rogue leader. T-Dog was capable of freezing one of the Swarm members; but if the Rogue leader was not incapacitated, the Swarm members could override the Captain's earlier desist orders, and through psychosomatic communication enlist the whole of the Swarm to battle T-Dog and Rebecca.

Answering Vasgus' question, the Captain exalted, "Yes, indeedy, Vas. The antennae that she was shoving up against is broken—not totally off—but hanging by a ligament, so to speak."

"You say it's not totally off, Cap?" Vasgus replied in a voice riddled with concern.

"Yeah, Vas. It's broken, but not entirely snapped off."

"What does that mean?" hollered Leapin' from the rear, exhibiting great distress in his voice. "It means that our hero dog, T-Dog, hasn't totally disarmed the Rogue," answered Vasgus, "however, she has gravely wounded it."

"Yippee...I think," Leapin' responded shyly after the initial burst of excitement.

"VeeGee," the Captain commanded, "give internal orders to T-Dog. Let her know the Rogue is wounded and to finish it off before it returns from a full-freeze state."

"Aye-aye, Captain," chimed VeeGee.

"And be careful," bellowed Vasgus. Johnny gave Vasgus a kind look of appreciation for his concern expressed for T-Dog.

Johnny watched through the viewing scope as his trusted mate neared the Rogue, and he held his breath in anticipation. T-Dog let out a "baroo" which startled Johnny, prompting him to pull back from the viewing scope. The guys immediately thought something bad had happened and rushed over to their Captain.

"It's nothing, guys," Johnny advised, eliciting a sigh of relief from both of his comrades. "She was just readying herself for the attack," added Johnny. "She'll often make some sort of sound from deep within as she gains strength."

"That means she's getting stronger," yelled Leapin' in a rising countenance.

"Yep, sure seems that way," assured Johnny.

After a few brief seconds, Johnny had regained his composure and reclaimed his position at the viewing scope, eager and yet hesitant to see T-Dog in action.

"Vas," Johnny beckoned, "what should T-Dog's battle plan be?"

But before Vas could respond, Johnny watched his trusted canine mate leap through the air into action. He saw T-Dog glide through the air in slow motion and come pounding into the antennae that was attached by only a fragment of a ligament on the Rogue. Just before contact, T-Dog let out a yelp releasing a quick blue-silver colored stream of freeze. Johnny saw the Rogue's antennae crystallize nanoseconds before T-Dog hit it broadside, full force. Splinters of the antennae ricocheted through the area, and T-Dog landed on the other side of the Rogue skidding on her side into the far wall with a sound thud.

"T-Dog!" Johnny exclaimed in fright. "Get up!" he added while backing away from the viewing scope. "Get up, girl," he hollered gripping his face in fear. "No, it can't be—not after all we've been through. It's not fair." Johnny was distraught seeing his dog fly so bravely through the air, impacting the Rogue with enough force to succinctly finish the job, only to lie motionless at the foot of a dark, grey wall—the outer boundary wall of the internal stacks.

"Captain," Leapin' beckoned solemnly. "What are our orders? What do you want Vas and I to do?"

᭣ 8 ᭢

Sweet and Sour Sage

Suddenly, a voice coming out of the distance within the stacks caught Johnny's attention, leaving Leapin's question hanging in midair.

"Ohhh…these big grasshoppers are really getting on my nerves."

The Captain strained his ears to hear the repetitive slapping of footsteps. *Hard-soled footsteps?* he wondered.

The Rogue is frozen; T-Dog lies motionless and she has soft feet anyway. Pausing momentarily to rub his chin in thought, *Rebecca Sage* popped into Johnny's mind, leaving a queasy feeling tumbling around in his stomach. Johnny kept looking and listening, his anticipation rising into anxiety as he tried to forecast the next events.

Then he heard from the inside, "If I have to hog-tie one more of those giant green grasshoppers, I'm gonna puke." Slap-slap-slap, went the sounds. "They're starting to really make me sick. All that sticky stuff that comes out those antennas is gross, not to mention stinky." Slap-slap-slap. "Oh…what have we here? One already down for the count? Oh, you poor green leaper, you."

The voice Johnny was listening to became pouty and sarcastic in nature. "Oh, somebody broke your antenna thingy off."

"Hey!" she shouted. "You're not dead, but you're not moving either. What's the deal? Obviously you can see because those big beady marbles for eyes are following my every footstep and move." Rebecca walked the massive circumference of the Rogue's sleeping head. Slap-slap-slap. "You probably can hear me too, can't you?" she asked glaring into one of the slow-moving, glassy eyes. "But you can't move, can ya?" Rebecca pondered out loud standing before the motionless green and gold-colored beast. "Now I wonder how this could have happened. Intriguing and weird, to say the least. Most definitely some of the weirdest things going on in here," she established confidently, rubbing her small, smooth chin and contemplating some more.

"Johnny!" she burst out, her voice rising suspiciously and drawn out in its drawl. "Johnny Rocket!" She stabbed poignantly, her tonal qualities bordering on accusation. "All of this, I'm certain, is because of him. Pahh!" she exclaimed in frustration. "He really gets me.…What's that?" she questioned, her voice softening a bit as she spoke.

Rebecca careened her sights over the top of the enormous bug lying helpless before her. Its translucent wing folded silently along the length of its striped and banded abdomen. Johnny heard the slap-slap-slap once again. "Oh no!" she cried out. "Johnny!" she once again exclaimed.

This time what Johnny overheard was not the cold, sarcastic voice of his rival but the voice of a gentle, concerned female soul. *What could have just happened that could have given Rebecca the gift of "heart"?* Johnny asked himself without moving his lips or taking his eyes out of the viewing scope.

"Gee whiz," Johnny exclaimed. *Could she be looking at my T-Dog? Girls always love dogs, and T-Dog is something extra special. Girls get that funny, sweeter-than-candy sound in their voices when they see a puppy. That would explain her sudden change in heart,* Johnny contemplated.

"Hey, Vasgus!" Johnny hollered. "Why can't I see where Rebecca is located through this viewing scope thing?"

"She's probably not within its internal camera fixation points, Captain," responded Vasgus promptly.

"But Vas, I can see T-Dog, and I think Rebecca can too," Johnny added inquisitively. "I need to see *her* and T-Dog," Johnny emphasized, turning to glare at his mighty Guardian friend.

"Let me see what I can do, Cap." Vasgus moved over to VeeGee's helm, placed his enormous hands on different controls, and began to move them about at a lightning-quick pace.

Johnny thought to himself, *No wonder he is so proficient in hand-to-hand combat. I've never seen anybody, or anything for that matter, move so fast.*

"Almost got it, Cap," Vasgus announced, hands slowing to a more traceable pace. "One more adjustment and you should be able to see inside the stacks anywhere you want. All you have to do is keep your eyes in the viewing scope and think about where or what you want to see, and the cameras will reposition themselves virtually to capture whatever image you're looking for."

"Virtually?" emoted Leapin'. "What the heck does that mean—'virtually'—Vas?"

Vas turned at the waist and peered down to address his little buddy. "It means, little one, that what you are seeing is a mimic of the reality that is inside the stacks."

"Wow, Vas! You continually amaze me," Johnny said looking up and around one last time before fixing his eyes in the viewing scope.

"My goodness, Vas," Johnny exclaimed upon fixing his sights into the viewing scope, "this is like something on one of my virtual reality 3D games, but far better and way more real!"

"Let me see! Let me see!" beckoned Leapin', positioned eagerly right by Johnny's side.

"Okay, okay, hang on, buddy. Ya don't have to push yer way in," Johnny gently scolded.

"Yeah, yer right, Cap. I'll wait my turn."

"That's okay, buddy. C'mon in, have a look." Johnny backed up a bit so Leapin' could squat in.

"Oh man, that's awesome," he said. "Whatever I decide I want to see—all of a sudden, I'm looking right at it, like I've been tele-ported there or something." Leapin' gave each of his cool, thin thighs a quick slap with the palms of his webbed hands—slap-slap. "Yet I remain here—not there. Vas, you are just as the Cap said—a real marvel."

"Oh my gosh!" Leapin' hollered, highly distressed. "Captain! There's T-Dog. I see T-Dog. She's just layin' by that wall." Johnny came scampering over. "Hey, wait a minute," Leapin' continued with a rising vigor in his voice. "Is that who I think it is? Is that Rebecca Sage standing right there too—standing right beside T-Dog? And...and...ohh...behind her is that Rogue thingy Vas made...layin' there, not moving too." By this time, Leapin' was really shook up by what he saw and turned away from the viewing scope in a daze.

Johnny shouted out, "I gotta get my dog!" snapping Leapin' from never-never land, back into the present. "Vasgus," Johnny beckoned.

"At your service, Captain," Vas replied wholeheartedly. "Your request is my command. What can I do for you?"

"You've done some things that have been pretty amazing," Johnny began, "always exceeding my beliefs in your abilities. Now, I have to get in there and get my dog," Johnny said, grab-bing hold of Vasgus' forearms.

"Hey, Captain," voiced Leapin' calmly from the distance, "first and foremost, I believe we must pray." Leapin' looked to the floor of the ship as if to check what he was saying, then continued boldly. "Yeah, pray. As I recall in all those times of obvious demise, you *always* got us together to pray—to seek God. And never did it fail that we skirted death through the Holy Spirit and Divine Intervention, and I don't see anything different about this situation."

"Wow, Leap, you're so right." Looking up toward the ceiling of the ship, Johnny said to the guys looking on, "My dad taught me to set things right with people, but he also told me it is good to set things right with God.

"Forgive me, Lord, for leaping around You. That's my dog in there, and I'm really worried about her. And I forgot to do the most important thing—to ask You for help."

Johnny looked over at his little buddy, Leapin', and said, "Thanks, Leap." Let's get together over here."

Johnny escorted each of the guys a few steps to his right. They all joined hands, and Johnny began to speak, "Our Father who art in Heaven…I love the way that sounds." Johnny became excited, overflowing with exuberance as he continued, starting all over, just so he could hear it again. "Our Father who art in Heaven, hallowed be Thy name…hmm, let' see," Johnny pondered rubbing his mouth with his right hand. "Thy Kingdom come, Thy will be done…" Johnny nodded his head in agreement, "…umm, in this Regatta," he paused smiling, "as it is in Heaven."

Leapin' softly interrupted, "What does 'hollow' mean, Cap?"

Johnny didn't answer his copilot at that moment but continued, "Father, I need Your guidance—Your help."

Looking at Leapin' Johnny said, "It's not 'hollow,' Leap; it's 'hallowed.' "

"That's what I said," pined Leapin', "hollow!"

"No, not 'hollow,' " Johnny explained, "but 'hallowed'—holy— the holy kind of hallow."

"Oh, I see," Leapin responded with a questioning look upon his face.

"C'mon guys, this is serious now," Johnny scolded, "just as serious as trying to get through an asteroid belt blind. That's my dog in there," Johnny emphatically voiced, pointing an outstretched arm toward the large computer bank running up and down the center of the ship, like a massive floor-to-ceiling bookshelf in the public library or museum—except this bookshelf did not hold books. This metal and glass shelf bank, complete with bright blinking lights and subtle ticking noises, held the deep inner thinkings of the Regatta itself.

Meanwhile, back inside the stack, Rebecca Sage heard a twitching noise behind her. Remaining transfixed upon T-Dog, she listened intently. She waited and listened...waited and listened...waited and listened. Silence was all she heard. It was an eerie silence because there were no sounds at all—not even of her own breathing or blood pumping through thousands of miles of her own veins.

Rebecca was afraid to move because it was sooo silent—*like death,* she thought. "Oooo!" she exclaimed, tightening her face and shaking out her arms like they had something on them. "Ick!" she added, like a bad taste or something repulsive had been added to her senses.

Twitch-twitch, again came the sound to her rear. Instantly, Rebecca knew what the twitching was this time around. But before she could surmise any plans, she was soundly struck upon the back, sending her into the far wall. Dazed but conscious, she could see the Rogue looming before her—its antennae glowing fiercely in front of her face.

She was so close to it she could smell its foul odor emanating from its mouth features. *Obviously, its mandibles,* she surmised. But she could not move, and dared not anyway. There was no way for her to gain any vantage in this struggle. She was already dazed with vision blurred, so she remained still, contemplating how long until her moment would come, and if she would feel anything in that moment.

"Baroo," harkened the sound of T-Dog, still positioned at the wall on her side but with head lifted up toward the Rogue.

"Bar-baroo," T-Dog repeated suddenly catapulting up to all fours. "Barrrooo!" T-Dog howled, glaring into the glassy beady eyes of the Rogue, firming up her muscular stance evidenced by the shifting to and fro and the thickening of her long white legs.

"Looks like somebody's threatening you, my dear bug," Rebecca scuttled sarcastically, gaining a half smile. As Rebecca painfully straightened herself up against the wall, gently cradling her abdomen, she saw the Rogue begin to dematerialize. "Huh?" she exasperated, adding a bewildered, "What?…Where?"

T-Dog added her own statement of confusion as she too witnessed the odd events taking place.

⌐ 9 ⌐

Divine Interference

Captain Johnny broke from the prayer huddle to reposition himself at the viewing scope. He spoke aloud to himself, "Just like Vas told me, I'll think about the what, where, and when I want to see, and this thing will take my vision there."

After a brief time, Johnny ripped himself away from the viewing scope hollering, "Vasgus, this thing's not working anymore. I don't see Rebecca, the Rogue, or even my dog. What's going on? Get over here!" Johnny commanded his big buddy, as a deep shade of red began to flood his usual olive-colored skin.

"Captain!" Leapin' beckoned. "Are you alright? Your face—I've never seen it look so...so red," Leapin' finished, a little perplexed by his Captain's appearance.

"Yeah," boomed Vasgus as he pushed by Leapin', lunging his way to the viewing scope, "the Captain will be fine in a moment. He's just really upset about his dog disappearing, and he's angry with me about it."

"That doesn't make any sense," Leapin' chimed. Addressing Vasgus, he continued, "You didn't do anything."

"Hey, guys," Johnny harkened, "enough of the fiddle-faddle. We got bigger things on our plate to contend with."

Leapin' noticed how the Captain's usual captainly demeanor had returned, replacing the ill countenance of earlier.

"Sorry, guys, for the way I've been behaving. It's just really hard when one of your best friends is in dire danger. I guess I didn't pass that test so well," Johnny finished.

"What test?" Leapin' asked.

"I remember my dad," Johnny began, "talking to me one afternoon about how tests will come into our lives, and their sole purpose is to mold and shape our character. Hopefully, we get built and shaped toward the Lord and not the other way. I guess what this showed me is how much I really do love that dog of mine, but more importantly," Johnny turned to Leapin', "you, Leapin', had to remind me to pray. I was already losing sight, and praying for Divine guidance hadn't occurred to me. My dad would always ask me what was occupying my mind more than God. And guys, please don't get me wrong…my love for the two of you far exceeds even that for my dog, Tasha—the poor girl," Johnny emphasized with a grimace.

Right at that very moment of contemplation, a bright sizzling sound startled the three comrades.

"What the…?" croaked Leapin'.

"Eeeh!" screeched the Rogue, sounding like thousands of rats scurrying away from flooding sewage waters in a concrete sewer. With additional clicking and chewing sounds, it slowly appeared just a few feet away from the exit door of the Regatta—a pair of yellow/green, glassy, oval-shaped, marble-like eyes followed by the rest of its oblong head with sharp mandible/pincers attached at the lower front.

"My God!" Johnny exclaimed in total respect and honor of the Lord's awesome power. "My God," he repeated, and added, "Lord, what has happened?"

82

Johnny had begun to make it a regular habit of communicating with the Most High during all his activities and doings. During his last early morning devotion, the Lord impressed upon his heart the necessity of communing moment by moment with the Lord, just as Adam did in the cool of the mornings when God came to walk and talk with him. However, this time Johnny's communication was not just pleasant talk. He needed the Lord's intervention on the behalf of all the guys.

"If that thing decides to go out that door…" Leapin' interrupted the Captain, "If that thing gets out that door, there will be no stopping it. It's gonna have its way with this planet if we don't do something."

"You're right, little buddy," Johnny confirmed. "Lord, make Yourself known here…even to the engineered bugs of the world. This Rogue threatening before us must know of Your reality…*now!*" Johnny commanded, throwing both hands toward the floor of the ship.

In the instant the Captain made this proclamation, a brighter, golden buzzing light began to envelope the Rogue. All three comrades in Faith took a step back, their faces aglow with bewilderment.

"Ahh," they sighed together.

"It's as if the thing is being burned up before us," remarked Leapin', looking to the Captain.

The sizzling, popping, and crackling noises coming from inside the glowing orb had an electronic sound to them.

"Sounds like the Rogue is getting its wires crossed," bellowed Vasgus from the rear, adding some light belly laughter at the end.

"I'd say it's getting more than that, Vas," Johnny added confidently. For Johnny knew well of his Father's Authority.

Johnny's premonitions of grandeur were soon shattered by Leapin' loudly voicing, "Hey, Captain, the glow is going away, and it looks like that Rogue thingy is still going to be here."

"Okay, boys," rallied Johnny, "it's gonna be our responsibility to fully dispose of this thing at this point."

Leapin' peered leerily into the Captain's eyes.

Johnny continued, "Our Father in Heaven is capable of doing anything He wants, but He also desires us to do our part too."

"You mean, God likes to work with us?" Leapin questioned, the buggy-look remaining in his eyes.

"Yep," answered the Captain with a slap on his thighs. "He sure does. Like I think I've mentioned before, the only reason He created us in the first place is for fellowship—fellowship with Him."

"I think," the Captain continued, "it's kind of like this…I like to hang out with you guys and you guys like to hang out with me, right?" Johnny pointed among the three comrades with fingers outstretched. "Just think if you were God, and you just made this great planet with all the other planets, and you had no one to talk to about it."

"Sounds kind of lonely," Leapin' countered.

"I agree," said the Captain next to Leapin'. Looking down at his little buddy with love, Johnny emphasized, "That's what I'm talkin' about—lovin' each other more than we love life itself and giving each other in deed or thought always." He finished with a big grin on his face, making him look like he was up to something.

"Father," Johnny began speaking once again, but very quietly. "You say I have been given a mighty sword for rightly dividing the Word, but I need Your might today in my hands." Intently looking at the palms of his hands, Johnny proceeded to bring them together in front of him in readiness to wield the sword.

When Johnny clasped and interlaced his fingers, Vasgus noticed the Captain's arms drop just a bit as if a weighty object had been placed upon Johnny's forearms.

"Captain!" Vasgus mightily exclaimed. But before Vas could utter anything further, Johnny slowly raised his clasped hands high above his head, arm muscles tensed. He paused and aligned his stance with that of his shoulders, wrists bent slightly aft. He then began to roar, first quietly deep down in his stomach, then out of his chest, fuller and louder, eventually opening wide his mouth. Johnny continued to roar so big, even Vasgus felt uncomfortable, as evidenced by his body language. Johnny could now clearly see the Rogue standing in full view because the bright, golden buzzing light that had enveloped the creature earlier had departed. Suddenly Johnny burst forth running straight at the Rogue at full speed. Then just as abruptly halted within arms' reach of the creature's port side.

Vasgus and Leapin' looked at each other, both wondering what crazed thought had captured their Captain. Leapin' began to step forward, but Vasgus shot out a thick arm to restrain him.

"But," Leapin' complained, grabbing hold of Vasgus' massive forearm pressing against his chest.

"No, little buddy. This is not your fight," Vasgus sternly warned.

At that moment, the two comrades in Faith witnessed a most spectacular thing. Johnny had dropped his clenched hands forward, toward the side of the Rogue, and after a display of firework proportions, the Rogue split in two halves.

In a shocking move, Johnny turned about and called his two friends forth to him. "C'mon guys. This is where we walk between the two halves of the enemy."

Johnny motioned toward the path with a wave of his hands. "Together, we mark a great and wonderful day. The comrades in Faith triumph once again!"

⊰ 10 ⊱
Victory!

The boys, arm in arm, strode between the halves of the Rogue, still sizzling and popping at the ends, startling little Leapin' as he walked through.

"Jeez, Cap, is that normal?" Leapin questioned, referring to the popping and sizzling noises.

"Well, Leap," Johnny began, "I figure it this way. We're probably never gonna be entirely ready for what the power of the Lord can do."

Leapin' acknowledged his Captain's statement with a gentle nod of his head and a grin of contentment across his thin lips. Vasgus evidenced an unwavering stance in Johnny's stature as he strode through, stepping in slow motion as the three remained side by side. The three turned about-face to look upon the enormity of the beast which spread out before them—two exactly measured parts—in perfect halves.

Finally, Johnny exclaimed with a bewildered look on his face, "Wow! Never thought I'd see this. Couldn't have imagined it in 10,000 eons, not even in Game-Kid, Rescue from Planet

Orbitor." Then Johnny stared at his hands, turning them palm up and palm down, then soundly clasping them together, delicately interlacing his fingers. He peered intently for some time at his clasped hands, waving them about as if he were wielding a sword again—waving overhead and before him. But nothing happened. Nothing could be seen in his hands.

"Hey, Cap," Vasgus summoned.

"Yeah, Vas, what is it?" Johnny responded with frustration.

"Maybe the sword's for battle only, Cap. Not something you can just conjure up, like foolish magic or something like that," Vasgus finished with a shrug of his house-sized shoulders.

"Maybe you're right, Vas," answered the Captain evidencing hints of despair through his body language. "Maybe this power is not for the taking; maybe it is for the giving only, given by the One who gives all life. He provided it—this gift of a sword of power, right when I needed it, and then it was gone."

"Yeah," Leapin' piped. "Vas and I watched you run at that Rogue thingy like you were possessed or something."

"Oh, little buddy, you don't know how right you are in what you just said," Johnny spoke, looking at Leapin' crouching before him. "As we prayed, I had this awesome feeling come over me. And I heard a faint voice too."

"Yeah?" Leapin' encouraged.

"Yeah," echoed the Captain. "A faint voice that I heard in my heart—words of guidance and encouragement were filling my whole head. It felt like someone was in there giving me directions on what to do to save us. It was really cool."

"Wow!" exclaimed Leapin'. "I wish someone was in my head telling me good things and how to do what you did, Cap. Cutting that thing in two was awesome."

"Pretty impressive for a human, Cap," Vasgus added bluntly.

"That's just it, Leapin'," Johnny revealed. "You *do* have someone within you, always desiring what is good for you to do. He even gives you the direction to do it; however, it's up to us to

88

decide if we're going to follow His good guidance or choose the lesser path," concluded the Captain.

"Jeez, Cap," Leapin' began, "sometimes you sound so full of good advice it boggles my mind. Where did you learn so much stuff? School?"

"No, Leap. I guess my dad and I spend a lot of time together when I'm not with you guys."

"Wow," Leapin exclaimed again. "That's really cool. Back at the pond on planet La Podia, we didn't know who our dads were."

"How's that?" Vasgus queried, furrowing his bushy eyebrows together, not understanding how someone could not know their own dad.

"On planet La Podia," Leapin' answered, "we were all just in the pond swimmin' around until we got old enough to be plucked out for labor training." Leapin' moved as if he were doing the breaststroke.

"He means 'slave labor training,'" Johnny emphasized.

"At the camps," Leapin' continued after the Captain interjected this truth, "they would pair us up with a friend who would share in the work detail."

"You mean," Johnny interrupted abruptly, "shackle you to another slave from the pond, using leg irons."

"Is that how you met this little guy?" Vasgus pondered.

"Yeah," Johnny answered. "I was landing on the planet La Podia for a systems check, and VeeGee located large bodies of water. I thought, *Hey, maybe it would be a great place to get a little rest before doing the systems check.* Well, let me tell you something, Vas. When I came over the top of a ridge, I found myself peering down into this valley that was full of murky, sludgy, gross-looking, and foul-smelling water as far as I could see. And at the bottom most pit of this giant watery pond, I saw thousands of little guys like Leapin' here." Johnny put his arm around his little friend. "And they all were tied together by the ankles.... Ya know, come to think of it, it's almost like the Jews and the Egyptians."

"What do ya mean, Cap?" asked Vasgus.

"Yeah, you're right, Cap," Leapin' affirmed, already seeing the analogy.

"Well, Vas, it's kind of like this—the Egyptians were enslaving the Jews in the mud pits, forcing them to make bricks."

"Why bricks?" barked Vasgus.

"So the Egyptians could build cities and thrones and idols to their own gods and for their own evil pleasures. Isn't that right, Cap?" Leapin' asked, looking over to the Captain after quickly jumping in on Vasgus' question.

"Yeah, little buddy. You basically got it," Johnny confirmed and continued speaking. "The Lord sent a man to lead the Jews out of their captivity and…"

"Just like you did for me, Cap," Leapin' fondly said, tightening his position next to the Captain.

"Yes, Leapin', I guess you could say…"

"What was that guy's name, Cap?" Leapin' interrupted again.

"His name?" Johnny restated.

"Yeah, Cap. Who was the guy that led the Jews out of captivity?" Leapin' restated his question.

"Umm," Johnny pondered, knowing full well that it was Moses who led the Israelites out of Babylon, but he lost train of his thought as he was trying to keep up with the quick vigor of Leapin'.

"It was Moses. Moses led the Jews out of captivity," Johnny answered.

"So, you're like a Moses, aren't you, Cap?" stated Leapin', looking up at his Captain.

"Jeez, Leap. Moses was a great man—a man who had face-to-face encounters with God Almighty. Please don't throw me in with comparisons like that. I appreciate your heart, little buddy, but be careful with comparing me—just little ole me—to any great Old Testament man of Faith," Johnny finished looking sheepishly.

Johnny was never known to be arrogant in his beliefs about himself, for he knew that anything good in him was a direct result of Jesus and the Holy Ghost.

Vasgus piped up from the back, "I think what our little friend is trying to say is that the way you led him out of captivity..." Vasgus paused and narrowed the distance between him and the Captain and then decided to rephrase his statement. "If that is what you did...just what did you do, exactly, anyhow, Cap?"

"Well," Johnny began, "I saw all those little guys chained together at the bottom of this watery pit..."

Vasgus cut in on Johnny's explanation and asked, "So, how did you know they were slaves and not just working together?"

"Good question, Vas," Johnny stated. "And one that is easily answered. You see, for every couple of little guys paired together, there were these big, tall people, or beings, or whatever they were, wearing black hoods and armed with long whips like the one I won at the county fair in the ring toss game."

"Like the one ya got over your dresser, Cap," Leapin' piped.

"Yeah, Leap, but these things were for real!" emphasized Johnny. "They were long and thick and braided all the way to the ends. I could hear the horrendous snapping of them every time they would shout at one of those little guy-pairs, forcing them to work harder or else they would 'get a cracking.'

"It pains me so because I can still hear the shouts of the captors followed by the squeals of the Lapodians. Even when they would do their best to work harder, they would still get whipped anyway. It was so obvious that they were trying as hard as they could, slipping and sliding, scrambling about in the sludge. That's when I couldn't take it anymore. After watching this for just a little while, I knew I had to do something. Even if I could help only one, it was gonna be worth the effort. Even as we do for the slightest or weakest of people, we do for Him." Johnny pointed an index finger proudly up toward the Heavens and then to his own heart, his eyes beginning to water with the thoughts and pictures of what he saw on that planet that day.

Johnny fought through his emotions and made one last statement. "I could only save one…"

Then Vasgus, although saved and loving God with all he knew how, bellowed, "Captain, tell me more of these 'captors' you referred to." His sense of empathy and compassion was still hard to come by.

"Well, Vas, I was positioned at the top of the ravine, hidden by the crest of the rock and overlooking the gallow of murk and mire that the Lapodians were being forced to work in. I decided to watch from afar until I saw the captors take a break. I figured they had to take a break sometime. Then I saw one of the captors dip a bucket-sized mug into the murk for him to sip out of. It was grey in color and all dented up. It even had a handle, like my mom's galvanized wash buckets. The tubular-shaped handle went the whole way across the top of this mug, and it happened to hit him smack in the face when he tipped it all the way back, making him more angry and aggravated with each drink he took. It really was ridiculous to watch—like a cartoon comedy or some slapstick comedy act. I would have been rolling on the ground laughing if it weren't for the seriousness of the whole situation down in the murky gallow.

"One by one, they all started drinking the dark-colored stuff, spilling it down their fronts as they drank. It looked like molasses; it was so thick and brown. They kept dipping their mugs in the pit where the little guys were stomping and working. And…like…" Johnny paused, "they were like…barking at each other or something."

"It's called Chaaga," Leapin' explained with remorse and sorrow permeating his voice. "It's pronounced ch-ah-ag-a, and it's made from the Aaga fruit!" Leapin's head bobbed up and back in order to punctuate and pronounce, "Aaga" correctly (ah-ah-ga).

"It's kind of like that real thick black beer from your planet, Cap, but this stuff is not meant to be drunk by anybody but the Lapodians—just us!" Leapin' emphasized the "us" with a closed-webbed fist brought across his torso to his left shoulder.

"Yeah?" the Captain was intrigued but carried on. "This stuff made them really insane, drunk-like, eventually falling over themselves and fumbling about.

"So that's the reason behind the enslavement of you little guys," barreled Vasgus. "You all had to make that drink for them," voiced Vasgus, referring to Leapin's people.

Johnny picked up where he left off in his tale. "After awhile, it was getting really nasty down there, and that's when I decided to *go for it.*"

Leapin' noticed the grief evident in his Captain's heart for Johnny's heart was to free all the Lapodians while the captors remained unconscious from the drink but just as the Captain freed Leapin' he heard more captors marching somewhere in the distance so Johnny using his better judgment, scooped up Leapin' in his arms and fled back to the Regatta. Leapin' looked lovingly up at Johnny and softly croaked, "Captain Johnny." Johnny turned his head to Leapin'.

"Captain Johnny," Leapin repeated, placing a palm on his smooth green-crested chest, "you saved me."

Rebecca gained a gentle grip about T-Dog's collar softly looking down at Captain Johnny's trusted canine friend, "well it looks like we're going to be partners in this dreaded place until some kind of answer or rescue can be had. At least that grotesque thing isn't in here with us anymore." Rebecca furrowed her thick eyebrows as her mind wandered wondering what might have happened to it.

"Barooo," answered T-Dog with a nod of her soft white head and moist black nose.

Addendum

Throughout this story, we've seen Johnny Rocket relying on the power and love of Jesus Christ, calling forth in prayer for the Holy Spirit's guidance.

If you too would like to know this same Jesus for the first time or recommit yourself, seeking deeper intimacy with the Father, there is no better time than right now, right where you are. All you have to do is pray…

"Father, I am sorry for my sins and wrongdoings, and I repent of them. Father God, come into my heart. I believe You were crucified and died for my sins. I believe You were buried and rose again. I believe You sent the Holy Spirit to be my guide. Now, fill me, Lord, with Your Spirit, the Holy Spirit. I will follow You all of my days. I love You, Lord. Thank You for Your sacrifice for me."

Now is the time for celebration. You will spend eternity with Jesus! Amen and Amen.

Loving the Lord,

Matthew Botsford

More Fiction
by Matthew Botsford

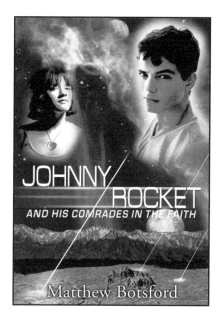

JOHNNY ROCKET AND
HIS COMRADES IN THE FAITH

Join a young boy's imaginative adventures in his intergalactic spaceship, The Regatta, with his "comrades in the faith," as they discover new worlds and civilizations while seeking to "save the world" as only a boy can imagine. Danger, sabotage, miracles, healings, and manifestations follow Johnny Rocket in his journeys, all the while revealing exciting, Biblically based moral realities.

ISBN: 88-89127-07-4

Order Now from Destiny Image Europe
Telephone: +39 085 4716623- Fax +39 085 4716622
E-mail: ordini@eurodestinyimage.com

Internet: www.eurodestinyimage.com

Additional copies of this book and
other book titles from
DESTINY IMAGE EUROPE
are available at your local bookstore.

We are adding new titles every month!

To view our complete catalog on-line, visit us at:

www.eurodestinyimage.com

Send a request for a catalog to:

Via Maiella, 1
66020 S. Giovanni Teatino (Ch) - ITALY
Tel. +39 085 4716623 - Fax +39 085 4716622

✳ ✳ ✳ ✳ ✳ ✳ ✳ ✳ ✳ ✳ ✳ ✳ ✳ ✳ ✳ ✳ ✳ ✳

Are you an author?

Do you have a "today" God-given message?

CONTACT US

We will be happy to review your manuscript for
a possible publishing:

publisher@eurodestinyimage.com